Margaret Tobin Brown

**Wanted a King**

how Merle set the nursery rhymes

Margaret Tobin Brown

**Wanted a King**
*how Merle set the nursery rhymes*

ISBN/EAN: 9783337259921

Printed in Europe, USA, Canada, Australia, Japan

Cover: Foto ©Andreas Hilbeck / pixelio.de

More available books at **www.hansebooks.com**

# WANTED—A KING;

## OR

## How Merle set the Nursery Rhymes to Rights.

BY

*MAGGIE BROWNE.*

Margaret Hamer

WITH ORIGINAL DESIGNS BY

*HARRY FURNISS.*

**SIXTH THOUSAND.**

NEW YORK

CASSELL PUBLISHING COMPANY

104 & 106 FOURTH AVENUE

# CONTENTS.

# WANTED—A KING.

THE BEGINNING OF IT ALL.

IT certainly was a beautiful screen. Merle always said that she liked the pictures on it better than all her story-books put together.

B

It was a screen covered with brightly-coloured pictures of all the Nursery Rhymes. On one side were Jack and Jill rolling down a hill, Bo-peep and Boy Blue, to say nothing of the Man in the Moon and the Old Woman who lived in a Shoe; and on the other side were illustrations of all the Fairy Tales.

The screen always stood by the side of Merle's bed, between the bed and the door; so that when Merle was in bed she could look at the pictures and say the rhymes over to send herself to sleep.

She had needed something to send her to sleep, too, since the day she tumbled. Merle dated everything from that tumble. Two months had passed since then, but Merle was still in bed. It had been a bad fall, so bad that at first every one thought that Merle would never again be able to run about and play like other children; but after a time the doctors said that if only Merle would lie still and wait patiently, some day she would be able to romp as much as she used to do.

Merle thought it was very easy to say " lie still and wait patiently," but she knew it was very difficult to do it when her head was so hot, and her body seemed full of aches and pains.

This afternoon, too, the pain was bad, and would not let Merle get any sleep.

She was staring at the screen, and gently singing to herself—

> " *Jack and Jill went up a hill*
> *To fetch a pail of water,*"

when there was a tap at the door, and an old gentleman came into the room.

"Uncle Crossiter," said Merle—for this old gentleman was Merle's uncle—" Uncle Crossiter, I cannot get to sleep. What shall I do?"

"Well, my dear," said the old gentleman, " I should say you had better let me move the screen away; you are not likely to go to sleep staring at those silly nursery rhymes. Such nonsense! Filling children's heads with such rubbish!"

B 2

"It is not rubbish, Uncle," said Merle, indignantly. "Please don't move the screen; I love to look at it."

But Uncle Crossiter took no notice of Merle, and only continued to grumble to himself.

"I should like to burn all the silly nursery rhyme books," he growled.

"That would do no good, Uncle," said Merle, quietly—"the rhymes are in the children's heads, and they will never be forgotten  *I* wonder what hill it was that Jack went up. It always says 'a hill,' you know, Uncle."

Uncle Crossiter started up. "Oh dear! oh dear!" he said to himself, "the child is wandering. There, keep quiet, my dear," he said to Merle; "I will send your mother to you."

"I am all right, Uncle," said Merle. "I won't talk about the nursery rhymes if you don't like them; but why don't you like them, Uncle?"

"Such silly nonsense, my dear!"

"Not nonsense, Uncle  they are beautiful. I do wish I had known Boy Blue and Bo-peep.

It would have been such fun playing with Bo-
peep's sheep," said Merle, quite forgetting that
she had promised not to mention the rhymes.

But it did not matter, for Uncle Crossiter had
disappeared. He was a matter-of-fact old gentleman, with no sentiment in him, and with rather
a short temper. He was very fond of his little
niece, and very sorry for her; but he did not
know in the least how to show his affection, for
he did not understand children at all, his one idea
about them being that they ought not to read
nursery rhymes.

Merle, however, did not notice that he had left
the room. She kept on talking to herself, saying,
" Bo-peep's sheep—Sheep's Bo-peep—Bo-sheep's
peep," and so on. How long she would have
gone on with this silly nonsense I do not know,
if she had not been startled by a voice behind
her, saying quickly,

" IF YOU WANT TO COME IN,

YOU MUST LEAVE YOUR BODY OUTSIDE."

# CHAPTER I.

"If you want to come in you must leave your body outside," said the voice again. "You need not be alarmed; I shall give you a ticket for it, and it will be quite right under my care."

Merle turned round astonished. The bed, bedroom, and screen had all disappeared, and she herself was no longer lying down, but standing—actually standing—in front of a turnstile.

Behind it was a little man, and he was evidently waiting for an answer to his question. Merle looked at him when she had recovered from her surprise. He was an ugly fellow—so short, really, that he only came up to Merle's shoulder, but as he wore a very tall pointed black hat he looked much bigger than Merle.

He was dressed all in black, for a long black

"'If you want to come in you must leave your body outside.'"

cloak covered him from head to foot. In front
of his hat were two red letters—two G's.

"G. G.," said Merle to herself; "what can
that mean?"

"Children are so rude," grumbled the little
man, who was still waiting for an answer, "they
cannot even reply to a question. I suppose this
child does not *want* to come in."

He turned round as he spoke, and was just
going back into his little ticket-office, when Merle
at last found her voice, and ventured to ask how
she should get on without her body.

"Children ask so many questions," said the
little man; "this child shall *not* come in."

This time he walked straight into his office
and slammed the door.

Merle felt very much disappointed, and rather
inclined to cry. She had no idea what she was
going in to; but, nevertheless, it was very annoy-
ing to be shut out.

Just then she saw a big, thin, yellowish-brown
thing—a thing rather like a very large stiff piece

of paper being blown towards her. It was curled round, and bent at the top.

To her astonishment, the thing stopped in front of her, and bending a little more, as if making a bow, said—

"Can I do anything for you, Merle? You don't know me, of course, but I know you very well. My name is Topleaf. I am—or perhaps I ought to say I was—the leaf that was on the top of the highest branch of the lime-tree in your garden. I have often peeped in at your window and nodded to you."

"I saw you this morning," said Merle, "and I know I said to mother that I should think you must be very lonely up there all by yourself. The other leaves have fallen long ago."

"It was lonely," said Topleaf; "but I could see a very long way, so that comforted me. At last I got my friend Mr. E. Wind to help me down, and here I am."

"But how is it you are so very big?" asked Merle. "You were not that size this morning."

" Ah, my dear! That shows how little you
know. Have you never yet heard that every
leaf tries as soon as ever summer is over to make
its way up to Endom ? "

" Endom ? " said Merle, " where is Endom ? "

" There," said the leaf, and he pointed over
the turnstile. " I thought you were going there,
perhaps, and I was glad, for a fresh child is badly
wanted."

Merle did not know what Topleaf meant by
the last part of his remark, so took no notice of
it, but said again, " But how did you grow so
tall ? "

" Ah, dear ! " sighed Topleaf, " I forgot all
about your question, and as usual, my dear,
wandered from the subject. Have you not
noticed how leaves never go anywhere straight,
and never keep to one purpose ? They run off in
a most flighty manner with the first breeze that
takes any notice of them."

As the leaf was speaking the little man
appeared at the gate once more.

"Hullo, Topleaf!" he said, "so you've arrived at last. I cannot say I am glad to see you. Are you coming in?"

Then he caught sight of Merle.

"That child still here?" he growled. "Disgraceful, I call it! Children are so obstinate," and without waiting to say another word to Topleaf, he shook his fist at Merle, and went back into his ticket-office.

"Who is that?" whispered Merle.

"That, my dear, is the evil spirit of Endom. He it is who has done all the harm to Mistress Crispin and her family. He it is who is the curse of all leaves," said Topleaf, and he rustled with rage. "If he could help it, we should never reach Endom. He puts every difficulty in our way. I had a brother"—here Topleaf lowered his voice—"but it is too sad a story to relate here. I only say that now he is a skeleton leaf." Topleaf was so overcome with his anger and sorrow that he curled up tightly.

Merle did not quite know what to do or say.

She was anxious to hear the rest of Topleaf's story, but did not like to disturb him. At last, to her great relief, he uncurled, and once more began to speak.

"I got here in spite of him," he said. "I conquered every difficulty, and so, of course, I grew. You know, my dear, that every time a leaf conquers a difficulty he increases in size. But we are wasting precious time. Come, let us go together into Endom."

Topleaf stood in front of the turnstile and shook himself vigorously.

Once more the little man appeared.

"So you've made up your mind to leave your body outside at last, have you?" he said, turning to Merle.

"Indeed I have not. I shall do nothing of the kind," said Merle quietly.

"But you *must!* you *must!*" said the little man angrily, stamping his foot. Merle noticed that the red letters on his cap grew brighter and brighter.

"All children must leave their bodies in my care. You mortals can only enter Endom in this way. Now then, if you are coming, come. Very well, I am not going to wait any longer," and he locked up his office and disappeared. Merle could not make out where he had gone to this time.

"Now what is to be done?" said she. "I did so want to go in—what a perfect little wretch he is!"

"My dear," said Topleaf, "you don't know what you have done. You have offended the mighty, the powerful

"GRUNTER GRIM!!!"

"Grunter Grim?" said Merle.

"Yes, Grunter Grim," said Topleaf. "I can't understand why he's acting as porter to-day: for no good purpose, I am quite sure."

"Well, it is done now, and cannot be helped," said Merle. "All the same, I must get in. Can't you help me?"

"I might, perhaps, if one of the Mr. Winds

would give
a helping
blow. The
worst of it
is, you are so
heavy. You
don't happen to
know anything
about the Wind
Family, I sup-
pose?"

"I am a-
fraid I don't,"
said Merle.

"Very well,
then ; I will do
the best I can.
Get inside me,"
said Topleaf.
He carefully
uncurled him-
self, and then

"'Get inside me,' said Topleaf."

getting behind Merle, slowly

curled himself up again round her, so that she
was completely hidden from sight.

"Now hold on tight!" shouted Topleaf.
"Here comes Mr. East Wind."

Then Merle heard someone whistle loudly,
and she supposed that must be Mr. Wind; next
she heard Topleaf slowly chanting these words :—

*"Blow, blow, blow,*
*Wind of the ice and snow ;*
*Just one gentle puff*
*Will be quite enough,*
*And over the fence we'll go ; "*

and then she felt herself lifted from the ground,
and carried into the air.

It was all over in a moment, for it was a very
short journey—only over the turnstile—and
Merle soon found her feet touching the ground
once more. Topleaf slowly uncurled, and Merle
stepped out.

She began to thank Topleaf, but he did not
take any notice of her. He just waited to see
that she was uninjured by the journey, and then
whirled away with his friend Mr. East Wind.

## CHAPTER II.

### WHAT MERLE FOUND IN THE BOX.

FOR a minute or two after Topleaf had left her, Merle stood perfectly still. Although the journey through the air had been short, it had also been quick, and had quite taken Merle's breath away.

"Well," she said at last, "here I am in Endom, I suppose. I wonder what kind of a place it is, and what sort of people live here? This is a funny kind of ticket-office."

As Merle spoke she was staring about her, and yet did not notice a long box on the ground. As she was leaning forward to peep in through the office window, her foot knocked against the box, and immediately a deep groan was heard.

Merle started back frightened, expecting to see the horrid little man once more, but he was not there.

"It must have been my fancy," said Merle.

o

But it was not, for by accident she knocked against the box again, and again came the groan ; and this time it was louder than before.

" Why, it comes from the box, I do believe," said Merle, when she had looked in the ticket-office and could see no one. " It comes from the box ! I do wonder if there can be anything or anybody inside ? "

" Anybody inside ? Of course there is. I'm inside," said a voice. " Whoever you are, let me out, oh do let me out!" The groans grew louder than ever.

" It is all very well saying that," said Merle, " but the box is fastened, and I don't know how to open it."

" Get the key, of course. It is in the office," said the voice, impatiently.

Merle ran quickly to the little door, and tried to open it, but it was fastened. Peeping in through the window to see if she could catch sight of any keys, Merle was astonished to see rows of paper-covered books standing on shelves round the walls, and she wondered what they were. However, there were no keys, so once more she returned to the unhappy creature in the box, who by this time seemed too tired to groan, and was only sighing faintly.

"I cannot get into the office," said Merle, sorrowfully; "and if I could, I don't see any keys hanging up."

"Hanging up? Whoever heard of keys hanging up? How would you hang them up?" asked the voice, angrily. "Didn't you see them standing on the shelves?"

"I saw some books on the shelves, but——"

"And what else would you have?" interrupted the angry voice. "If you want to open this box, you must find the right book, and read the proper rhyme, of course. You don't seem to know what a key is. What is the key to your arithmetic book like?"

Merle felt there was something wrong somewhere, but she didn't quite know where. She felt, however, that arguing wouldn't release the

c 2

poor creature from his sufferings, so she hastened
to say—

" But the office door is fastened."

" Then there is nothing else for it—you must
sit on me—I will do my best not to hurt you,"
said the voice; " but if I don't get out somehow,
I shall certainly die."

" You won't hurt me," said Merle, " but if I
sit on you I am afraid I shall hurt you. However, I will do as you wish."

She sat down on the box, and the groaning
grew louder than ever. Presently, however, it
altogether ceased. There was a very loud noise,
as of something bursting, and then Merle felt
herself shot up high into the air.

The box-lid seemed to have tossed her as if
she had been sitting on the horns of a bull. It
was startling, and she did not recover from her
astonishment for some time. When she did, she
found herself sitting on the ground. Staring at
her, standing upright in the box, was a very tall
boy, dressed in a very old-fashioned coat, with

" Merle felt herself shot up high into the air,

large round buttons. Round his neck was a big, wide, stiffly-starched frill, which Merle thought must be decidedly uncomfortable.

"Thank you very much," he said, bowing politely. "*What a good boy am I!*" he continued.

Merle looked somewhat astonished.

"My name is Jack Horner," he said, bowing again, "and I——"

"Sit in a corner," interrupted Merle, eagerly, "eating a Christmas pie; and you put in your thumb——"

The boy frowned and looked very cross, but Merle did not notice it, and went on talking—

"And pulled out a plum, and said——"

But the boy could bear it no longer, and began shouting at the top of his voice, "To be a good boy I will try——"

"That's quite wrong," said Merle, indignantly. "You made a very conceited remark—you said, 'What a good boy am I!'"

"But I didn't, I didn't!" said Jack Horner.

"It was Grunter Grim who told the fairy who makes the Rhymes that I said so, and now I have to keep on saying—'What a good boy am I.'"

As he said this he got very excited, waved his arms about, and sat down suddenly in the box. At once the lid closed down, and he was a prisoner again.

Merle released him as quickly as she could, but begged him not to do it any more, as she did not enjoy being shot up into the air.

"I hope you are not hurt," said Jack.

"Not a bit, thank you," said Merle—"I only feel rather giddy. Would you mind telling me why you got into that box at all? It surely isn't very comfortable?"

"What a good boy am I!" said Jack, angrily. "Comfortable!—Got in!—Do you suppose I got in? It was Grunter Grim who shut me up, and even now I can't get right out."

"Why, you are a regular Jack-in-the-box," said Merle, beginning to laugh.

"There," said Jack, indignantly, "that is

another thing Grunter Grim has done. He not only puts me in this box, but he tells the fairy who makes the Toys about it, and then the children hear of my disgraceful situation. He is horrible! I suppose you thought I did nothing all day but sit in a corner and say, ' What a good boy am I ?' "

"Why, do you do anything else?" asked Merle.

" Do anything else!" screamed Jack. " Why, I am the porter of Endom, and Grunter Grim shut me up to-day, so that I couldn't let you in. He is nothing less than a monster!"

" He does seem to have treated you badly," said Merle, sympathisingly. " I must say I am very glad to know that you are not really so conceited as I always thought you were."

" What a good boy am I !" said Jack, very dolefully. " Yes, I know that sounds conceited, but you understand now, don't you, that I only said, 'To be a good boy I'll try?' It is all Grunter Grim's fault."

" He must be dreadful! " said Merle.

" But you will save us all, I hope," said Jack. " Go up the hill and talk to mother : she will show you what to do——"

He was about to tell Merle more about his mother, when it suddenly began to grow dark, as though a black cloud were coming down from the sky to the earth.

" Run, run! " shouted Jack. " Grunter Grim is coming ! " and he quickly sank down into his box.

Merle did not wait to be told twice, but ran quickly away from the office. She never stopped, and never once looked behind her until she found herself in front of a large black house.

# CHAPTER III.

" It is a queer house," said Merle, aloud : " a very queer house. It's such a funny shape."

Merle was quite right : it was a queer house, and a very peculiar shape. To begin with, the house was certainly not built of bricks; then it was very long and low, and what Merle called " uppy-downy." The windows were in such funny places—and as for the front door, why, there was none. The only way to get into this house seemed to be to climb up a rope ladder which hung down from the middle of it. Part of it, too, was entirely without a roof, and another part was so narrow that Merle felt quite sure she would never be able to get into it. She noticed that there was a bright shining piece of brass fastened on to the narrow part, and when she looked at this more closely, she found that it was evidently used as a

door-plate, for on it was written, in very plain
letters,

MISTRESS CRISPIN.

"I suppose that is the name of the person
who lives in the house?" said Merle; "but what a
funny door-plate: why, it has a big hole in the
middle! And what a very, very, very funny
house!" Merle walked right round it twice.
"It is not a house at all," she said, and she
walked round it again. Then a bright idea came
into her head—"Why, why, why," she cried,
"it's nothing but a big shoe!"

And so it was—a great big shoe. The rope
ladder was the shoe-lace, and the brass door-plate
the shoe-buckle!

"Now," said Merle, in a satisfied tone, "the
next thing, of course, is to find the old woman and
the children.

"*There was an old woman who lived in a shoe.*

"Standing on tiptoe, she managed to peep through one of the little windows."

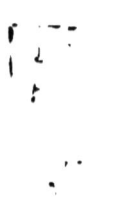

Of course, this is the shoe, and I suppose the old woman's name is Mistress Crispin."

By standing on tiptoe, she managed to peep through one of the little windows that was let into the side of the shoe. She could see what looked like a very comfortable little room inside. There was a fine big fire burning brightly, and on the fire were two huge pots, which were evidently bubbling and boiling with all their might and main, for the smoke was coming from them in big clouds.

There was no one in the room, but there was evidently some one in the house, for Merle heard a very great noise of beating and banging.

" Oh dear!" said Merle, greatly distressed, " she must be at the '*whipped them all soundly*' part, I should think, by the noise. I must go and stop her."

She ran quickly round the house to the rope ladder, and, after some little trouble, managed to climb right up it, and get inside the shoe.

She found herself in a tidy little room, evidently a sleeping room, for there were a number of little beds, as many as could be got into the room, against the wall. Merle thought she heard a noise in the next room, so she hurried on.

Directly afterwards she found herself in the room she had seen from outside; but now there was some one in it.

By the side of the fire was a tiny little old lady. She was stirring something in the pot with one hand, and with the other was wildly waving a big birch-rod, nearly as big as herself. As she waved she kept knocking the chairs and tables that were within her reach, so that she made a good deal of noise.

"What I expected," said Merle; "this, of course, is Mistress Crispin."

The old lady turned as Merle pronounced her name, and said, in the very crossest of cross voices,

"So delighted to see you, my dear!"

Merle was most astonished.

" Do keep out of my way, darling," said the old lady, angrily, " or I shall be obliged to beat you."

Merle quickly got outside the door, and only popped her head in to talk to the old lady. The voice and tones were so very cross, and yet the words were so kind, what could it mean?

" Where are the children?" asked Merle, at last summoning up all her courage.

Poor Mistress Crispin looked crosser than ever, though the tears rolled down her cheeks as she said,

" Gone, my dear, gone! They simply could not stand the beating and the broth."

" Why, how wicked of you!" said Merle. " How cruel of you to drive all your children away from you!"

" Oh, my dear! you don't understand, or you would never talk like that. Come and stir this broth whilst I fetch something soft to beat, so that I shan't make such a noise, and then I will tell you all about it."

D

Merle ran at once, and took the spoon from the old lady's hand. Mistress Crispin turned away directly, so as not to be able to beat Merle; but although she tried her hardest, she could not help hitting her twice.

Merle looked rather angry, but before she could say anything the old lady kissed her, and ran to fetch a pillow from the bedroom.

Then when Merle was comfortably settled in a chair, and Mistress Crispin had once more taken the spoon to stir up the broth, she began her story.

" A long time ago I lived happily with my family in this comfortable roomy house, I had so many children——"

" That you did not know what to do," nterrupted Merle.

" On the contrary, my dear, I always knew what to do. I never had a minute to spare, I was so busy ; but I did not mind that, for I loved my children, and they loved me."

" But if you loved them so much, why

did you whip them all soundly and send them to bed?" asked Merle.

" If you will wait a minute, I will come to that," said Mistress Crispin. " Well, as I was saying, we were once all very happy, but troublous times came to the country, and discontent seized the land. Grunter Grim deceived us, and by deceiving us got power over us."

" All the same, I don't see why you gave those poor children broth," said Merle. " I don't like broth myself, especially without any bread."

" Oh, my dear!" said Mistress Crispin, in the crossest of cross voices, whilst the tears rolled down her cheek, " I didn't give them broth. I cooked the dinner as usual, and a very good dinner it was—roast beef and plum pudding. Well, I cooked the dinner, and put it all on the table, and told the children to begin, while I went out just to wash my hands. When I came back—I hadn't been

D 2

away more than a minute—I found all the
children fighting and quarrelling——"

" Oh, how dreadful ! " said Merle.

" Indeed it was. When I asked them what
was the matter, they said they wanted to know
why I had given them such a dreadful dinner."

" What peculiar children ! How funny of
them not to like beef and plum pudding ! "
said Merle.

" That was what made me angry; and
without stopping to think," said the old woman,
beginning to cry again, " I fetched out the birch-
rod and began beating them."

" And they quite deserved it," said Merle,
very decidedly.

" No, they didn't : it was all a mistake. Let
me finish my story," said poor Mistress Crispin.
" In the middle of the bother, when they were
crying, and I was beating, it grew dark, and in
came Grunter Grim. He laughed a horrid laugh.
' I am glad you like my broth,' he said; ' you
shall always have it; and since you are so fond

of beating, you shall always beat,' and then with another laugh he went away."

" What did he mean by talking about broth?" asked Merle.

" Why, don't you see," said Mistress Crispin, "it was he who had changed the beef and plum pudding into broth."

" Oh, how wicked of him!" cried Merle.

" Next day," continued the old lady, " I was still obliged to speak angrily and beat the children, and every day after, until at last they ran away and left me. And now, although I am all alone, I can do nothing but beat the children that are not there, and make this horrible broth."

" What a shame!" said Merle. " I wish I could punish Grunter Grim."

" You can," said Mistress Crispin.

Just then a girl popped her head in at the window.

" Good morning, mother," said she. " May I come in ?"

" Don't, dear, don't," said the old lady,
angrily. " You know I must beat you if you
do. Have you found the tails?"

" No, mother, not yet," said the girl. " I
dream of them every night, but in the morning
I find my poor sheep still without them."

" Are you Bo-peep?" said Merle, eagerly. " I
have long wanted to know you. I have heard
of you so often," and she began to sing—

> " *Little Bo-peep has lost her sheep,*
> *And doesn't know* —— "

But she stopped suddenly, for she saw the girl
look very angry, and then run away from the
window.

" There, of course, she is offended," said
Mistress Crispin; " it was very rude to remind her
of that insulting story. But perhaps you do
not know who stole the sheep's tails. You must
get her to tell you some day."

" Is she your daughter?" said Merle, hoping
to change the subject.

" Of course she is my own dear daughter
Bo-peep. You have much to learn yet about my
family, and I want you to do it quickly, for
then you will help us. Can you not see that it is
Grunter Grim who is our great enemy ? He
has done all the harm, and worked all the
mischief."

In her eagerness and excitement, the old lady
had gradually spoken louder and louder, and had
drawn nearer and nearer to Merle.

At last she was so close that her birch-rod
actually touched Merle, and at once, though poor
Mistress Crispin tried to stop herself, she began
to beat Merle. Each time she apologised most
humbly in the angriest tone of voice.

" I beg your pardon," she said, stamping her
foot. " I am so sorry. I hope I don't in any
way hurt." Thwack, thwack, went the birch-rod,
and Merle began to make her way to the door.
" I don't want to hurt you," continued the old
lady, " but I feel one of my bad attacks coming
on. Please, oh, please, do get out of the house!"

She followed Merle, beating her all the time with the birch-rod, and begging her pardon, until Merle once more reached the ladder and got out of her **way.**

# CHAPTER IV.

As soon as she reached the bottom of the ladder, Merle stopped to think. The question was, what ought she to do next?

She was very anxious to find out all about the Rhymes and Grunter Grim, but she certainly could not go back to Mistress Crispin, it was too dangerous. She shut her eyes tightly. When she opened them again, to her surprise, Mistress Crispin's house and the road to the turnstile had entirely disappeared, and in front of her rose a high hill. At the foot of the hill was a sign-post, and on it was written " A——— Hill."

" That's the name, I suppose," said Merle; " but why don't they put it in full? What is the use of giving only the first letter of a name ? "

" That shows you don't know anything about it," said a voice quite close to her ear.

Merle turned round quickly, and was surprised
to see a girl and boy, carrying an empty pail
between them, walking beside her.

The boy and girl did not seem at all
astonished to see her, however.

" Well, you've come at last ! " said the boy,
crossly. " It was time you did, though I don't
suppose you'll be any better than all the others."

The girl took no notice of his remark.

" The name is put like that," she said to
Merle, " so that other children shall not have to
waste their time as we do, fetching and spilling
water."

" Excuse me," said Merle, very politely ; " but
are you Jack and Jill ? "

" Of course," said the boy, " and we are going
up Argument Hill to fetch a pail of water."

" Oh, Jack," interrupted Jill, " you shouldn't
have told her the name. Now every child will
find out where the hill is, and will follow our
example, and try to carry pails up it. You
know what a bother it was to me to persuade

the Rhyme Fairy to leave the real name out of the story-books."

" I can't help it," said Jack, " I forgot."

All this time they were gradually climbing the hill—indeed, they had almost reached the top.

" You're always forgetting," said Jill.

" 'Tis your fault," said Jack.

" It's yours," retorted Jill.

" Oh dear, please don't quarrel," said Merle, stepping between them. But she was too late, for just then the hill seemed somehow to rise up, and in a minute Jack fell, and began rolling down the hill. As for Jill, she didn't even wait to fall, but at once lay down, and rolled after Jack.

" Just what I expected," said Merle. " I only hope Jack's crown is not quite broken."

When the two reached the bottom, they picked themselves up, and Jack immediately pulled some plaster out of his pocket, which Jill fastened on his head, and then shaking hands, they once more started to carry the pail up the hill.

They seemed to be friends again, and to be talking quite kindly to one another. Merle sat down on the ground, and determined to wait until they arrived.

" Don't quarrel again," she shouted.

Jack nodded and smiled, and Jill put her finger over her mouth to show that she was not going to talk at all.

It was no good, however, for, just as they reached Merle, Jack kicked a stone. At once Jill turned round, took her finger from her lips, and said angrily,

" Do be careful."

" It was your fault," said Jack.

The words were scarcely out of his mouth before down he tumbled, down sat Jill, and away the two went rolling to the bottom of the hill.

" This is all very well," said Merle, " but if they are going to do that for ever, of course I can't stop here."

She only waited to see that neither the

brother nor sister was badly hurt, and then
picking herself up, walked on over the top of the
hill and down the other side.

She had not walked very far before she came
to a narrow, straight lane, with a high hedge on
each side. It looked dismal and lonely, and
Merle was just coming to the conclusion that
she would not go any further, when she caught
sight of a bit of blue petticoat and a black shoe
peeping out from underneath the hedge, half-
way down the lane. She walked quickly to the
place, and there found a girl lying fast asleep
under the hedge, and she at once recognised
her as the one who had come to see Mistress
Crispin.

" *Little Bo-peep fell fast asleep,*" said Merle,
gently, for she did not want the girl to be
offended again.

As she said the words, however, Bo-peep sat
up and rubbed her eyes.

" Come, my pretty lambs," she said, sleepily.
" I am glad indeed to see you again."

Merle stared at her, and wondered whatever she was talking about. She was just going to ask

a question, when Bo-peep suddenly stood up and burst out crying.

"They are not there," she sobbed, "and I dreamt so plainly that I heard them bleating."

"Never mind," said Merle, kindly. "I'll

help you find them. Who stole your sheep,
dear, was it Grunter Grim?"

"Of course it was," said Bo-peep; "but come,
let us hasten," and she quickly wiped her eyes
and stopped crying. "If we are sharp, we shall
be in time for the meeting."

"What meeting?" asked Merle.

"The meeting of the Family," said Bo-peep.
"Every night at twelve o'clock we are all
free for one hour. Until one, Grunter Grim has
no power over us, and we are able to leave our
work. Then we meet together and discuss our
plans for overcoming the tyrant."

"But can I come?" said Merle. "Won't he
be angry if he knows I am there?"

"He won't know," said Bo-peep. "I will get
you in, it is a secret meeting."

She took hold of Merle's hand, and at once
everything became dark. Then she heard a clock
begin to strike twelve, and then another, and
then another, until all round her the air seemed
full of the sound of striking clocks. Some had

deep notes, some silvery ones, but the noise was
so great that Merle put her hands over her head
to keep out the sound. When she took them
away again, she was no longer in the narrow
lane, but in a large room.

# CHAPTER V.

It was a very large hall indeed, and quite unlike any hall that Merle had ever seen before. Instead of having a raised platform at one end for the speakers, and rows of chairs in front of it for the listeners, nearly the whole room was taken up by an enormous platform, and there was only one row of chairs in front of it. Even this, as Bo-peep told Merle, was not really necessary, for every one always wanted to talk, and no one to sit down and listen.

"Well," said Merle, "there will be some one to listen to-day, so I will sit on one of the chairs."

But Bo-peep would not hear of it, because she said if Merle sat by herself Grunter Grim would notice that a child was present.

There were several people already on the platform when Merle and Bo-peep took their seats.

E

The clocks were still striking; but whenever any clock struck for the twelfth time, some new visitor arrived.

Merle soon recognised her friend Mistress Crispin sitting quietly in a chair, and not even trying to beat any one. Jack and Jill were sitting side by side, laughing and talking happily together, although Jack's head was tied up in a big red handkerchief, and Jill's arm was in a sling.

Merle soon found out, too, who all the others were, for each one wore a small ticket, on which a name was written.

There was little Boy Blue, as wide-awake as could be, and next to him the Man in the Moon. In the front row of chairs Goosey Goosey Gander and Miss Muffet, sitting side by side, were talking away to Pollie Flinders and Tom, Tom, the Piper's Son, and making a great deal of noise. Miss Muffet looked such a dashing young lady, that Merle wondered how it could have happened that she should have been frightened by a spider.

Just as the last clock finished striking, Mother
Hubbard came hurrying into the hall, followed by
a dog and quite a number of people, a cobbler, a
baker, a tailor, and many others. Merle was
just going to ask Bo-peep who these people were,
when Mistress Crispin stepped forward and began
to speak.

" My children," she said, " it must be fully
twelve by the earthly clocks; what is the time by
the nursery clock ? "

Directly she asked the question, each one
present produced a dandelion clock, and began
solemnly and seriously to blow upon it. Mistress
Crispin counted aloud " One—two "—and so on,
up to twelve, and by that time the seeds were
scattered in every direction, and she and the
others held dandelion stalks only in their hands.
At the same time, the hall, which Merle had
thought very badly lighted before, became
brilliantly bright. It seemed as though the stars
had come down from the sky, and had fastened
themselves upon the walls, but really there were
E 2

no stars. Each dandelion seed had turned into a bright shining lamp.

Then once more Mistress Crispin began to speak.

" Merle," she said, " listen to our wrongs, and help us to make them rights. You can do it if you will. You know my story, now listen to some of the others."

She quickly sat down, without wasting more time, and at once Bo-peep, Humpty Dumpty, the Man in the Moon, and Boy Blue all rose together, and began talking very quickly.

Merle could not in the least understand what they were saying. She only heard one name, which they each used several times, and that name was Grunter Grim. After they had been speaking a minute, Mistress Crispin held up her hand, and they all stopped and sat down.

" There, Merle," she said, " you know now how wrongly and wickedly Grunter Grim has treated us all. It saves so much time if four of the children speak at once, and it does not matter

if you do not hear each word, for you can judge
of the tyrant by his deeds. You have seen the
result of his actions, and after that, words make
no difference."

"But how can I send him away?" asked
Merle.

"Choose us a king," said Humpty Dumpty.

"Have faith in yourself, and defy him," said
Boy Blue.

"Do anything you like, only do it quickly,"
said Mother Hubbard.

"Yes, indeed," said the cobbler, the baker,
the tailor, and all the other people who had come
with Mother Hubbard, "do it quickly."

Merle stared at them all. She did not in the
least understand what they were talking about.

"A king?" she said at last; "what do you
want a king for?"

"Oh dear! oh dear!" said Mistress Crispin,
"we must go back to the beginning of all things,
and explain matters to her. Well, Merle, we had
a king who was able to keep Grunter Grim in

order. At that time Grunter Grim had no power over us, he could only growl and grumble to himself."

"Then the time came," said the Man in the Moon, taking up the story when Mistress Crispin paused to take breath—"then came the time when our king finished his reign, and because Grunter Grim deceived us, we had not chosen a new one. We could not agree which of the claimants was the right one, and so we quarrelled."

"That's the whole point," interrupted Boy Blue, "we quarrelled. You see, Merle, as long as we were all contented Grunter Grim had no power over us; but as soon as we quarrelled he just took the power into his own hands, and since then he has treated us shamefully."

"But how silly of you to quarrel!" said Merle.

"It is easy enough to say that now," said a girl who had not spoken before.

Merle did not have to ask who she was, for she saw at once by the ticket fastened on her dress that she was "Mary, Mary, quite contrary."

"Hush, hush, Mary!" said Bo-peep, "please don't be rude to Merle."

"But why don't you stop quarrelling?" asked Merle.

"Because as long as Grunter Grim has power over us, we can't help it," said Mistress Crispin.

"If we only once got up that Hill without disagreeing," said Jack, "we shouldn't tumble down, of course, but it isn't all our fault. Grunter Grim makes us fall out, and fall down too," he added, rubbing his head.

"If this goes on much longer my arms will be too much bruised ever to get well again," said Jill, dolefully.

"It isn't all temper that makes us quarrel, Merle, don't you see that?" said Mistress Crispin.

"Besides," put in Bo-peep, "if you spent your whole day looking for sheep's tails, I don't think you would be sweet-tempered."

"Now, Bo-peep! don't get cross," said Mistress Crispin, "that is no good. Our time is

nearly up, it is a quarter to one. Cannot some
one tell this child what she is to do to help us?"

"I will," said Goosey Goosey Gander,
drawing herself up, and stretching out her
feathers. "Merle, listen. The next time you
see our common foe, you must stand up and defy
him, and banish him from the land. You *can* do
it, if you *will*. Then, when he has gone you
must choose a king for us."

"I will do my best," said Merle, "but I'm
afraid I am not much good."

"I never expected you would be," said Mary,
Mary, quite contrary.

"Do be quiet, Mary!" shouted Boy Blue.

"She can give her opinion if she likes," said
Jill.

"Yes, of course," said Mother Hubbard.

"Of course, of course," called out the cobbler,
the baker, the tailor, and the others.

"Oh, please don't begin quarrelling now,"
said Mistress Crispin. "It is only five minutes
to one, and then——"

But the hall was beginning to grow dark, although the dandelion seed lamps were shining as brightly as ever. Merle took hold of Bo-peep's hand, for she felt rather frightened. But Bo-peep did not take any notice, for she seemed to be gradually dropping off to sleep. Then Merle looked at Mistress Crispin, and she was no longer sitting still, but was moving her hands about, feeling for her stick.

It grew darker and darker, and somehow it seemed to Merle as if some one outside the hall were shouting. She felt sure she heard some voice in the distance—what could it mean? She was getting more and more frightened. She turned again to Bo-peep, but Bo-peep was fast asleep, and evidently dreaming, for from time to time she turned in her sleep and muttered something about her sheep. Darker and darker!

Merle at last could bear it no longer, and she started to her feet with the intention of getting down from the platform and running out of the hall. But instead of running away, she stood perfectly still, for there shining at the end of the hall were the fiery letters " G G." They came closer and closer to her, and she knew it was Grunter Grim. Then she remembered all that Goosey Goosey Gander had said to her, how she was to defy the tyrant, and banish him from Endom. She summoned up her courage and began to speak.

" I de——" but she got no further, for just then the clocks outside began striking one, and as the red letters came closer and closer to her, she heard a voice saying—

> " *Once more in strife now ends your hour,*
> *Once more 1 have you in my power.*"

All thought of finishing her sentence and banishing Grunter Grim went out of Merle's head. She was terrified.

As the fiery letters came closer to her, she screamed at the top of her voice, "Topleaf— somebody—help ! help ! "

She quite expected to feel Topleaf's arms round her, but instead, something seemed to come between her and the horrible letters, and she heard beautiful music, and a soft voice singing a lullaby gently and slowly.

Merle knew the tune, but somehow she could not think of the words. Gradually the lullaby grew louder and louder, and the voice appeared to come nearer and nearer. At the same time the fiery letters on Grunter Grim's cap became fainter and fainter, until at last they faded away. Then the darkness lifted, and once more it became light.

# CHAPTER VI.

## G—— G——.

By the time that Grunter Grim's cap had disappeared, and the darkness with it, Merle's courage had returned. As soon as it was quite light again, she stood up and prepared to speak to Bo-peep; but, strange to say, Bo-peep, Mistress Crispin, Jack and Jill—all the Nursery Rhymes, in fact, and even the Hall—had entirely vanished. Merle could scarcely believe her eyes, but it was indeed the case. She herself was the only thing that had not disappeared.

All this time the lullaby was still going on, though now it was fainter—so faint that Merle scarcely noticed it, as she had so many other things to think about.

She was now standing out of doors, in the middle of a road, or rather at a place where four roads met.

" ' Look up, and you will see.' "

Not far from her stood a sign-post, with each of its four arms pointing towards one of the four roads.

Merle walked up to the post to see what was written on it. On the arm pointing to the road on her right was written—

G—— G——.

Merle felt quite frightened when she saw the dreadful letters, and was going to hurry on to see if anything better were written on the next arm, when she heard some one speaking to her.

" Look closer before you run away, my dear," said the some one.

Merle could not in the least understand where the voice came from, but she once more looked at the sign-post, and then found that there were other letters besides the two G's. Carefully she spelt it out, and found, after some trouble, that

To Grumbling Greatly

was written there.

"That doesn't sound very inviting," said Merle.

"Of course not," said the some one again; "look at the next."

On the next Merle discovered—

To Gliding Giddily

written in the same way as the first, with the G's large and the other letters small. Very disappointed, she turned to the third, and on that was written, just in the same way—

To Gossiping Grandly.

"This is too provoking," said Merle. "I shan't trouble to look at the other. That horrid Grunter Grim is everywhere. I hate the sight of those wretched letters G—— G——."

"Don't lose your temper, my dear, that never does any good," said the some one.

By this time Merle was quite angry.

"I wish you would show yourself, whoever you are," she said.

"Look up, and you will see."

Merle looked up, and to her surprise saw that
it was the sign-post itself that was talking to her.
It was not like an ordinary sign-post, for right at
the top, some distance above the arms, there was a
head. It looked as if it were only carved wood,
but it was quite as able to talk as Merle herself.

"Don't apologise," said the post, "you are
only making the mistake that other people have
made before you. They only look at a sign-post;
if they talked to it they would get much more
information, for have we not stood in our places
for a very long time? And do we not know a
great deal more about the country than we can
possibly put on our arms?"

Merle determined that she would no longer
make the mistake of only looking at the post,
and decided to get as much information as she
could. She was rather ashamed of herself, so she
said, humbly—

"Would you mind telling me why you have
those horrid letters G G on your arms?"

"Do you think I wrote them?" said the

F

sign-post, very indignantly, and he got so excited
that his arms shook. "Is it likely that I should
write such stuff?"

"Then I suppose Grunter Grim has power
over you, as well as over every one else. Did he
write them?" asked Merle, hoping to calm the
excited post.

"Of course he did," said the post, sulkily.

"What do they mean, please?" said Merle;
"surely there isn't really a place called 'Grumbling Greatly.' I wish you would tell me, because
I must go somewhere, and I don't know which
way to go, and you said I was to talk to you, because you know so much. Please help me."

The sign-post had been getting calmer and less
sulky as Merle spoke, and when she reached the
end of her long speech he said, quite mildly—

"Well, I will help you. Now listen. A long
time ago, when we had our own king, I was a
sensible sign-post, with proper directions written
on my arms."

"Then you quarrelled with some one, I

suppose?" said Merle, "and so Grunter Grim got power over you. It is the same story over again."

"Not quite," said the post, sadly, "I did not quarrel with any one. I suffer because of other people's wickedness. Every one *would* quarrel with me."

"That is pretty much the same thing, isn't it?" asked Merle.

"Not at all, not at all, but it had the same effect. Grunter Grim came and spoiled all my arms, and now every one goes the wrong way."

"Well, help me to go the right. What does 'To Gliding Giddily' mean?" asked Merle.

"'That means really, 'To Jack and Jill's Hill.' Jack and Jill spend all their time 'gliding giddily,' you know, so instead of writing on my arms ' To A—— Hill,' Grunter Grim has put ' To Gliding Giddily.' He likes that name, partly because it misleads every one, and partly because he can use his favourite letters, G G."

"Oh, I understand now. Then, 'To Grumbling

Greatly,' let me think—now, what does it mean?
I know—the way to Mistress Crispin's, of course,
and 'To Gossiping Grandly' is the way to the
Hall."

" That's right, my dear," said the post. " You
really are a clever girl, though you have only two
arms."

" Why, of course I've only two arms," said
Merle. " However many did you expect me to
have ? "

" Four, of course," said the post. " How can
you point each way if you haven't four? Why,
you wouldn't be any good at all on a cross road."

Merle felt that this was unanswerable, and
decided to turn the conversation, so she said—

" You haven't told me now which way I am
to go. It's no use my following those three
roads, for I know all about them."

" Try the fourth, then," said the post.

Merle remembered that she had not even
looked at what was written on the fourth arm of
the sign-post, so she walked round to it.

It was quite as difficult to understand as the other three, for on it was written—

B—— B——.

" That is not much help; I don't know what that means. Who is B—— B——? " said Merle.

There was no answer. Merle looked up at the sign-post, but it seemed to have lost the power of speech—it only stared at her.

" Well, this *is* stupid," said Merle.

The sign-post took no notice, but the arm pointing to B—— B—— shook slightly. It might have been the wind, it might have been fancy, but Merle certainly thought the arm shook. She at once decided that at any rate she would go along the road leading to B—— B——, and try to find out who B—— B—— was. Directly she had come to this conclusion she heard the voice singing the lullaby once more. It seemed, too, as if some one were holding her hand, and she felt as if she

were floating along in the air rather than
walking.

The farther she got from the four roads and
the sign-post, the louder the lullaby grew and
the firmer her hand was held, and at last the
lullaby stopped, and a voice said—

"Merle, I am delighted to see you. Will
you come in and see the claimants to the throne?
for you must find a king of Endom."

## CHAPTER VII.

### IMAGINARY TWINS.

MERLE looked about her. She could not see any one, and, what was worse, she could not see anywhere to go in. But she was getting used to queer things by this time, so she simply said—

" Show me the claimants, and I will do the best I can."

At once she saw in front of her a long low building. It had not been there before, or rather, Merle had not seen it there before; but she was not at all surprised, and walked straight towards it. The door opened, and Merle found herself in a long room. It was almost entirely filled with babies' cradles.

Babies' cradles of every description! Some quite grand ones, trimmed with rows of ribbon and lace, so grand that you would never have thought of giving them such a simple name

as cradle, but would have at once decided that
they were "bassinettes." Some quite ordinary
basket cradles, some old-fashioned wooden ones
that had evidently been used for more than one
generation of babies, and some not proper cradles

"Some quite grand ones."

at all. One was an old tin bath, another a big
basket, and another a wooden box.

Yet they were all—the grand ones, the
ordinary ones, and the funny ones—they were

certainly all cradles, for each one contained a
baby. There was perfect silence in the long
room, although there were so many children and
not a single nurse—perfect silence, absolute
quiet!

Merle at first thought that all the babies must
be asleep, and, fearful of waking them, stepped
very quietly up to the cradle nearest to her, and
peeped in.

She was most devoted to any baby ; she loved
the whole baby race, as every girl should do,
and, in fact, as every right-minded girl does.

Well, Merle peeped into the first cradle.
It happened to be one of the grandly trimmed
ones. In it was lying a very small, very thin,
very pale, but very clean baby. Any one who
was not fond of babies would have said, " What
an ugly baby !" Merle only thought, " That
poor baby looks ill !" The baby, however,
seemed happy enough—it was not asleep, but
was lying contentedly on its back. As soon as
it caught sight of Merle it gave a delighted crow,

and at once from every cot of every kind came a baby's joyful crow or coo.

You know, if you know anything about babies, how enjoyable it is to hear one happy, comfortable baby coo. Just fancy what a glorious thing it would be to hear dozens and dozens of perfectly happy babies gently coo with delight.

Merle smiled, simply because she couldn't help it, and then she laughed, at what she did not know. Then she looked once more at the baby in the gorgeous cradle, and noticed for the first time that there was a ticket fastened to one of the curtains. On the ticket was written—

The
Finest Baby
in the World.

Merle looked twice, she thought she must have made a mistake; but no, there it was plainly written, " The Finest Baby in the World."

She was rather astonished, for she felt sure that she had seen finer babies many a time.

In the next cradle—the tin bath one—lay a very bonnie baby, also wide-awake and perfectly happy. This was quite a different-looking baby. It had rosy cheeks and curly hair, though rather a dirty face. It really was a fine baby. Merle saw a ticket fastened to this cradle, and when she looked at it, she saw written on that too, " The Finest Baby in the World."

Then she looked at the next cradle, and on that was another ticket with exactly the same words on it. She looked at another, and another, and another—it was just the same all the way round—every baby, pretty or plain, clean or dirty, thin or fat, each one was labelled, " The Finest Baby in the World."

Merle stood bewildered. What could it all mean?

"It is simple nonsense!" she said aloud. "There can be only one *finest* baby in the whole world."

",That's just the point," said the voice Merle had heard when she had left the sign-post—the voice that had invited her to look at the claimants. Merle turned round, for now there was something more than a voice. Standing close beside her was a small boy who looked about three years old, but who spoke as if he were very much older.

"Just it," he repeated decidedly; "that's just what we want to find out, which is the finest?"

Merle stared at him, amazed.

"Where did you come from?" she said at last.

"I came in long ago," said the boy, "but I was weak. When Grunter Grim told me, as he told you, I could only come in by leaving my body outside, I left it."

"But you got it back, I suppose?" said Merle.

"No, I didn't," said the boy, indignantly,

"not my own body. This one doesn't belong to me. I really am a girl, and I was ten years old when I came to Endom, and when I wanted to go out again Grunter Grim said he had given my own body away, and this was the best he could do for me. That's what he does—gives back the wrong bodies, and then down in that stupid world, every one is astonished because big people are often cowards and little people brave, some girls more like boys, and some boys more like girls. It is easy enough to explain it if they only knew the reason why."

"I suppose it is Grunter Grim's doing," said Merle, thoughtfully.

"Of course it is," said the boy. "Children get to Endom, leave their bodies in charge of Grunter Grim, and enter without them. Of course they are unable to help the poor Nursery Rhymes, and when they go away disgusted Grunter Grim gives them back wrong bodies. I am not going back until I get my own property. He knows where it is."

" But how will you get it—er——" Merle
stopped and hesitated. "Would you mind
telling me your name? It is so much easier for
me to talk to you, if I know your name."

"My name? Certainly," said the boy. "It
is Thomas Muriel."

Merle stared.

" Don't you see," he continued, "Muriel is
my own proper name, but Thomas is the name
of this body that I am now in."

Merle looked still more amazed, but the boy
was getting so indignant that she did not like
to say any more about his name—so asked how
he thought of getting his own body back again.

" Why, *you* will help me to do that—any one
of these babies could answer that question," said
the boy.

Merle did not understand how she was to
get the boy's own body for him, but he seemed
to know all about it and the babies too, so she
thought she would probably find out in good
time.

" Now then," said Thomas Muriel, when Merle stood perfectly still, without saying anything, " now then, be quick and decide."

" What am I to decide? " asked Merle.

"Which really *is* the finest baby in the world. You said yourself that there could only be one."

" But why do you want me to decide such a difficult question at all ? "

" Because we want a king," said Thomas Muriel. " Before the last king finished his reign the Rhymes were all quite happy, but when he was forced to resign——"

" Why did they make him resign if they were all so happy? How very silly of them ! " said Merle. " Oh, I am sorry ! I never thought before that Nursery Rhymes could be silly."

Poor Merle was so excited that she almost began to cry.

" Wait a minute, my dear, wait a minute," said Thomas Muriel, not in the least disturbed by Merle's excitement. " You don't know what you are talking about. The last king was not

forced by the Rhymes to resign, but he lost all
his power. He got to be able to talk and walk."

" Talk and walk?" said Merle.

" Yes, talk and walk. What are you
astonished at now? Don't tell me that you
don't know about the Kings of Endom —you can't
be as ignorant as all that."

" But I am," said Merle. " I don't know
anything about it. Do explain."

At first, when Merle made this dreadful
confession, Thomas Muriel looked horrified, and
turned round as if he were going to leave her,
but Merle looked so much ashamed of herself and
so humble that he relented, and once more
began to speak to her.

" A long time ago, Endom, which you know
means Nurserydom or Nurseryland, was the very
happiest land in the whole world. All the
Rhymes were merry, jolly, and contented, and
never even thought of quarrelling. The finest
baby in the world who could not walk or talk
was always made king."

" Who made him king?" asked Merle; " who chose him ? "

" Who chooses your king," said Thomas Muriel—" I mean your King of England ?"

" But we haven't a King. We've a Queen," said Merle ; " and she isn't chosen a Queen, she's born it."

" Well, it was exactly the same with the Kings of Endom," said Thomas Muriel, getting rather impatient, " **they were** born it. You can't make a baby the *finest*, it has to be born the finest."

" Well, then, I don't see what was the difficulty," said Merle. " Why is there no King of Endom now ? and how is it that all these babies are labelled, ' The Finest Baby in the World ? ' Who gave them their labels?"

" Their mothers, of course," said Thomas Muriel. " Don't you see, when the Rhymes couldn't decide for themselves which was the finest baby in the world, they sent messengers into the world to find out what the mothers

G

thought.    And each mother thought her own baby the finest."

" They might have expected that," said Merle.

" Of course," said Thomas Muriel, " but that doesn't settle the question.   It is very easy to be clever now, but then at the time Grunter Grim deceived the Rhymes——'

" How ? " asked Merle.

" Twins," said Thomas Muriel.    " Twins were at the bottom of it all."

" Twins ! " said Merle ; " twins ! "

" Yes—don't you believe me ?   I think you are very stupid."

" I think you are very rude," said Merle.

It was beginning to grow dark—but the two children were so busy talking that they did not notice it.

" Of course I believe you ; but I can't understand what twins had to do with it."

" Not real ones," said Thomas Muriel, very crossly.—It grew darker.   " Imaginary ones.'

" Now you are talking simple nonsense," said Merle. " Imaginary twins—that's rubbish."

By this time it was quite dark, and Merle could no longer see Thomas Muriel. All at once it flashed across her mind that darkness meant Grunter Grim. Immediately her anger vanished.

" Thomas Muriel," she began, " don't let us quarrel."

All at once the babies began to coo, and it began to grow light.

For a little time it was quite bright in the room once more—but when Merle looked round for Thomas Muriel, he had disappeared, and she was alone with the babies.

G 2

# CHAPTER VIII.

"Now, what is to be done?" said Merle. "I shall never find out quite all about the Kings of Endom. Grunter Grim is evidently doing his best to stop me. I expect he made Thomas Muriel cross. All the same, I do wonder what he meant by talking about twins. Whatever could twins have to do with the Kings of Endom? Merle was talking aloud, standing in the middle of the big room; but as she asked the last question she walked slowly towards one of the cots.

To her surprise, the baby in the cot immediately began to talk, and not only that baby, but all the other babies. Every baby in the room was talking hard. The funny thing was that though the babies were using just the same baby language of coos and gurgles and a-goos that they generally use in the world, Merle perfectly understood what they said, and they evidently understood each other.

Merle listened with the greatest attention, for the babies were answering her question about the twins, and telling her the true story about the Kings of Endom. As you cannot understand baby-talk, I must tell you in proper language what the babies said to Merle.

Listen, then—

" The Finest Baby in the World was always made king, and before he was able to walk and talk properly, his successor was chosen. Well, it happened once that Grunter Grim was admitted to the meeting at which the future king was to be chosen. Now you must know that the king's name was always announced by the Messenger from the Leaves—for the Leaves know which is the finest baby, as they hear all that goes on in the world, and only come to Endom when they are old and need rest When the name of the future king was given, Grunter Grim got up, and asked very quietly and innocently if the Rhymes

were sure that their friends the Leaves had fixed
on the finest baby, for he knew that the one
named had a twin brother.

" This remark at once upset the meeting. No
one ever thought of finding out if what Grunter
Grim said was true. They know now that it
was false. But at that time they immediately
began to discuss what should be done.

" There was, of course, great disagreement.
Some thought there ought to be two kings,
others declared that idea absurd, but all were
agreed that where there were twin-babies, one
could not be very much finer than the other.

" Finally, the meeting broke up in the greatest
confusion, without any king having been chosen.

" At the next meeting, Grunter Grim spoke
still more strongly. As a result, there was more
disagreement. At the next, it was worse. Then
he suggested that the mothers of all the babies
should be asked which was the finest, and, as you
know, that only caused greater trouble. Time
passed on, and still no king was chosen.

" Then there was not only discontent at the meetings, but before them and after them. The time was taken up in discussion and argument, and nothing was done.

" At last the king was obliged to resign, and no successor had been chosen.

" On that day the last meeting was held. Grunter Grim was present, and when the assembly broke up in confusion, he shouted, ' I will give you a king ; I will be your king myself. Henceforward, obey Grunter Grim !' Then all was dark—that was the day on which Mistress Crispin's dinner was changed ; that was the day on which Jack and Jill, as they went up the hill quarrelling, were thrown down ; that was the day on which Bo-peep's sheep's tails were cut off, and the Man in the Moon burnt his mouth. Every misfortune, every trouble that has come to the Rhymes, dates from that day."

This is the story, as the babies told it to Merle.

When they had finished speaking, Merle

waited quietly for two minutes, then nodding to
them, she said—" Thank you ; at last I understand all about it.   Now I must set to work to
find a real king for Endom, and he ought to be
a king for all time, so that there may never
be any more disputes and quarrels."

After she had made this little speech to the
babies, she bowed, gave them each a kiss, and
then walked out of the room.   She felt sure that
the future king of Endom was not there, and
made up her mind that she ought to begin
looking somewhere else for him without wasting
any more time.

She passed through several rooms, filled with
babies and cradles, and at last came to a very
small room.   At first she thought that this was
quite empty, for there seemed to be nothing in
it ; but then she noticed that though there was
nothing actually in the middle of the room,
round the walls there were glass cases.   When
she looked closely at these cases, she saw that
they were filled with rows and rows of letters.

"Very curious," said Merle. "I wonder whose letters they are, and why ever they keep them here?"

Then she looked still closer, and then gave a loud cry of aston-ishment. It was so loud, that if any one had heard her I am sure they would have come quickly to the rescue, for they would have thought that she was in pain. How-ever, no one did hear, so that it did not matter. After her first surprise,

"There were hundreds of them."

Merle seemed to know exactly what to do. She opened the glass case and took out one of the letters, and then she opened it.

Perhaps you may think it was very wrong
of Merle to open somebody else's letter. So it
would have been, but this was not some one
else's; it was her own, for it was addressed to
Merle.

And this was not the only one. Every letter,
—and there were hundreds of them—every
letter in those cases was meant for Merle to read,
although they were not all actually addressed
to her.

On some of the envelopes, " To any Human
Child who can read " was written, and on others,
" Let any child who comes to Endom read this."
On a great many Merle's own name was written
in very plain letters.

Well, Merle opened one letter, and this is
what she found inside—

> *" If you would banish Grunter Grim,*
> *Have not the slightest fear of him."*

" I've heard that before," said Merle;
" there's nothing new in that. What is in the
next ? "

She opened another letter, and found the very same words in that. Then she opened another and another, and about twenty others, and every one was exactly the same.

At last she opened one of the letters directed "to any Human Child who can read," and there she found something diferent, for in that the following words were written :—

> " *If you'd help us, quickly bring*
> *Unto Endom Endom's king.*
> *Find his name, you'll then find him.*
> *Who has got it? Grunter Grim.*
> *Search his house, you'll find at last,*
> *'Tis written down, but sealed up fast."*

" Grunter Grim's house," said Merle; " why, I haven't seen that; I didn't know he had a house. I will go at once; but perhaps I had better finish reading the letter first, as there may be something more in it."

There *was* more in it, and this is what Merle read :—

> " *If you ask who wrote it down—*
> *'Twas one who never wore a crown.*
> *But the monster Grunter Grim*
> *Stole the secret—shame on him!*
> *If you'd get it back again,*
> *Remember this, I write it plain—*
> *When Grunter Grim says ' Yes '—say ' No ' ;*
> *When he says ' Come'—then quickly go ;*
> *When he says ' Fly '—be sure to stay ;*
> *When he says ' Stop '—then run away.*
> *Defy, Deride, Desist, Deny,*
> *Heed not a growl, or scowl, or sigh.*"

Merle read it all through twice, and put it in her pocket. At last she really understood what she was to do.

She wondered very much who had written all these letters. She was leaving the room when she remembered that she had not yet opened one of the letters that had " Let any child who comes to Endom read this" written on it. She thought she had better do so, and she walked back to the glass case, took out a

letter, and opened it. This was a very short
letter, there were only a few words written on a
big sheet of paper.

> *" Beware my fate,*
> *I thought too late,*
> *I'm Kate."*

" Whatever does that mean ? " said Merle. " I
had better look at another."

She found in the next—

> *" Do as the letters say—*
> *Be careful to obey,*
> *Or you will fail in the way*
> *That I did—Maggie May."*

" I wonder if these are from children who
have been to Endom, and then have been unable
to defy Grunter Grim ? I wonder what has become of them, and what will become of me ?
Well, I can but do my best."

So saying, Merle shut the glass case, picked
up all the opened letters, made a little heap
of them, and then walked out of the room. She
was determined to do her best, determined to

try to follow the directions in the long letter
which she had put in her pocket.   As she left the
babies' house she repeated aloud the last words—

> *"Defy, Deride, Desist, Deny,*
> *Heed not a growl, or scowl, or sigh,"*

**and** somehow she found them very comforting

# CHAPTER IX.

### A WINDING WAY AND A CROOKED HOUSE.

OUTSIDE the house, Merle found herself standing
facing a broad pathway, with a high hedge on
each side of it. She walked a little way down
the path, and found that it divided, and that
several small paths led out of it. Each road
was closed in by high hedges, so high that Merle
could not see over them, and could only wander
aimlessly on and on.

The paths twisted and turned, wound in and
out, crossed one another, curved, and sometimes
suddenly came to an end.

It was fatiguing work, and Merle soon began to feel very tired. Her feet ached, her
legs ached, and her head ached. For she was
beginning to feel not only tired, but worried and
frightened, for it was evident that she had lost
her way. Then it began to grow dark, but

she was not at all disturbed by that, for she
knew that darkness only meant Grunter Grim.
And when she remembered Grunter Grim, she
took courage, and began to walk more quickly.
She felt sure that this crooked, roundabout way
must be connected with him, and she felt con-
vinced that she would soon find herself at his house.
She was quite right.   The road grew narrower,
the hedges higher, and, almost directly after, Merle
found herself in front of a dark, dismal house.

Like everything else belonging to Grunter
Grim, the house was black.   It was not straight
up and down.   Like the way to it, it was very
crooked.   The walls leant on one side, they
seemed as if they must surely tumble down soon.
The few windows—and there were very few—
were scattered about, as it seemed, anyhow.
One end of the house was very high, and looked
as if there might be six or seven storeys, and the
other end was quite low, only one storey high.
Everything about the house looked crooked, and
wrong, and uncomfortable.

Merle was not at all surprised at this, however, for she did not expect to find anything pretty or straightforward in connection with Grunter Grim. She looked about a long while for the door, and at last discovered it high up, in what seemed like the top attic. You would scarcely have thought that a door could be put in such a funny place, but this evidently was a door, for there was a knocker fastened to it and a door-plate, but certainly it was not the least bit of use to any one inside or outside the house.

Merle looked about to see if she could find any sign of a side-door or a back-door. They were quickly found, but they were in such queer places that nobody could use them. Since there was no door for her to enter, Merle decided to try a window. She noticed one, quite close to the ground, in the one-storeyed end of the house, and quickly walking to it, she peeped in.

She could not see very much inside, as it was dark, and it was only a little window. After peering in for a few minutes, Merle gently

H

tapped. There was no answer, and no sign of any movement inside the house.

Merle knocked much louder; still no sign. She knocked again, and this time called, "Grunter Grim, Grunter Grim, are you in?"

Still there was no answer, so Merle pushed the window to see if she could open it, but it was fastened very securely.

She did not know at all what to do, so she pulled out her letter of directions, to see if she could find out anything from that.

She opened it out, and began to read aloud from it—

"*If you'd help us*——"

Merle got no further, for she heard a sudden click. She quickly turned round, but she could see no one. She began reading her letter again. Just as she got to the words "Search his house," she happened to look at the window, and, to her amazement, she saw that it was actually opening, as it seemed, by itself.

For a moment Merle stood still, overcome

by astonishment, and then she stepped lightly over the low window-sill, and in at the open window.

She fully expected to find Grunter Grim waiting to receive her, but when she got inside the little room she found no one there, and as soon as she was out of the way, the window quietly shut down.

Merle found herself in a very queer place. The room had no wall-paper—at least, if there was one it was quite impossible to see it, for each of the four walls, as well as the ceiling, was covered with something that looked like a kind of rough woollen material. It was a very light colour, nearly white in some places.

Merle thought it looked rather peculiar, and so went up and touched it. It felt like wool, it *was* wool, but Merle found it was all in loose pieces. She pulled one of the pieces apart from the rest.

" Why, it looks just like——" she began, and then she stopped. She remembered that

H 2

Grunter Grim might be in the house, and might hear her remarks.

"It looks like sheep's wool," she continued, in a whisper. "I do believe it is a sheep's tail."

She looked again. Then she very nearly shouted, "Of course, of course, these are Bo-peep's sheep's tails. I've found them."

She was so pleased with her discovery that she determined to examine the rest of the room very carefully.

It contained a perfect mine of treasures. Evidently it was Grunter Grim's store-room, where he kept everything he had stolen from the Rhymes. In one corner Merle found Little Boy Blue's horn.

"Of course," she said, "this explains it. Little Boy Blue couldn't very well blow his horn when Grunter Grim had it here."

In another corner were some gardening tools, and these were labelled, "Johnny's Tools." Merle stood before them for a long time,

wondering who "Johnny" was. Then, all at
once, the rhyme came into her head—

> "*See-saw, Margery Daw,*
> *Johnny shall have a new master.*
> *He shall have but a penny a day,*
> *Because he can't work any faster.*"

"Of course Johnny wasn't able to work quickly
when Grunter Grim had his tools."

Merle was continuing her examination of the
room, when suddenly she remembered her letter.
She had forgotten the directions, and instead of
looking for the packet in which the future king's
name was written, she was amusing herself.
She put Johnny's tools down, and began soberly
and seriously to hunt in every nook and corner
for the sealed packet.

She left the little store-room and went into
the other parts of the house, but found no sign
of the packet.

At last she returned to the store-room, and
once more began to hunt there. She noticed
something black in a very dark corner that she

had not seen when she looked before. She
picked the something black up, and found when
she shook it out that it was a long cloak.

"Grunter Grim's cloak," said Merle, with a
shudder.

Again she looked in the corner—there was
something more in it. This time she pulled out
Grunter Grim's big pointed hat. Merle looked
at the front of it, wondering if the fiery letters
would be there, but there was not a sign of
them.

Scarcely thinking what she was doing, Merle
wrapped the cloak round her and put the big hat
on her head. She began to feel quite queer
immediately. A change seemed to be taking
place in her character.

Before, she had felt happy, peaceful, and
interested, for she was always a very contented
girl, even down in the world, where she had
to lie in bed all the time. As soon as she put
Grunter Grim's clothes on, however, she felt
herself growing very miserable. Somehow she

felt dissatisfied and unhappy, and yet she could give no reason for it.

If she had given way to this feeling, there is no knowing what would have happened; but she was a sensible girl, and she made an effort, and pulled herself together, shook herself, and said very earnestly—

"Now then, be sensible, Merle."

At once she began to feel stronger, very much stronger. The uncomfortable feeling had almost disappeared, and she was about to take off the cloak and hat, when she heard a very loud noise. The whole house seemed to shake—the sheep's tails waved in the air, Boy Blue's horn stood up and made a bow, the window opened, and Merle saw a dark little man jump into the room.

It was Grunter Grim, come home at last!

# CHAPTER X.

## HOW MERLE FOUND THE STOLEN PACKET.

It was Grunter Grim, but for the first minute or two Merle did not recognise him. He looked so much smaller, so much meaner, so much less formidable without his hat and cloak, that Merle did not feel the least bit frightened of him, and was only amused.

He was evidently in a bad temper, for he was no sooner safely inside the room than he began stamping and storming and raging.

Merle was in a dark corner, and he did not notice her at first, so she silently listened to him.

"Jackanapes, Jingles, and Jaguars!" he muttered. "Was there ever in this stupid world any one so stupid, so silly as I? Shall I never learn how very risky it is to go out without my

cloak and hat? Fortunately, no one has found
me out this time."

Merle shrank farther into her corner.

" But I had a quick run for it. That Thomas
Muriel nearly caught me. And if he had, by
the toes of all the sardines, what would have
become of me? He knows the secret only too
well."

The little man was dancing with rage, up
and down the room. He looked so small, yet he
had such a big voice and talked so quickly.
Presently he looked into the corner. He had
evidently come to the conclusion that he would
not be without his clothes any longer.

" Beetles, Biscuits, and Bandboxes !" he
cried, " has any one been here? Can my cloak
and hat be gone? No, they must be in the other
room." And he bounced out of the door.

Merle came out of her corner and listened.
She could hear him running and jumping all over
the house, calling and shouting all the time.
Presently, before she could disappear, back he

came into the room.  Directly he caught sight of
her in his hat and cloak, he gave a furious yell, a
wild leap into the air, and then began dancing up
and down the room—talking and shouting the
while.

In spite of the cloak and hat, which had made
her feel so brave and strong, Merle began to think
that she was just the least little bit frightened.
You see, she knew only too well what dreadful
things Grunter Grim had done to other people,
and she did not know, that as long as she kept
the cloak and hat on, he could do nothing to her.

The little man stormed, the little man raged,
and then he began to threaten.

" I'll lock you in a dungeon !" he shouted, at
the top of his voice.  " I'll make you into mince-
meat!  I'll, I'll——"

He hesitated what to say next.  Then, as he
saw the colour going from Merle's face, he
screamed—

" Now will you give me back my cloak and
hat?  Say ' Yes,' at once ! "

"Grunter Grim comes home."

Merle lifted her hand to her head to take off the hat—but she still hesitated, and it was well she did. The little man noticed it, and repeated his last words.

" Say ' Yes,' at once ! " he shouted, stamping his foot, " and give me the hat, and you shall go."

But these words reminded Merle of her rhyme—

*" When Grunter Grim says ' Yes,' say ' No,' "*

and plucking up all her courage, Merle pulled the hat down more firmly on her head, and said—

" No, I won't give you your hat and cloak, Grunter Grim ! "

She fully expected to find herself blown into the middle of next week or that something dreadful would happen, and she shut her eyes tightly. When she opened them again she was still in the little room, and Grunter Grim had not gone, but he seemed somehow to be completely changed. He was standing silently in one corner. He looked no longer angry and threatening, but dreadfully, painfully miserable.

He was shivering and shaking from head to foot, and big tears were rolling down his cheeks.

Merle felt inclined to cast the cloak and hat before him, if only to cheer him up.

" What is the matter? Are you very cold, Grunter Grim?" she asked, in a gentle voice.

" Cold! I am shivering so much that I cannot keep still," said Grunter Grim, in the mildest, meekest, softest of voices. "Oh! have pity on me, and give me back my cloak. Have you never been cold yourself? Will you not have some mercy?"

As he spoke Merle began to think she must be a very bad girl to steal some one else's cloak, and let them shiver for want of it.

She looked at Grunter Grim as he stood before her crying and shaking, then a tear rolled down her own cheek, and giving a big sigh, she raised her hand to unfasten the cloak. As she did so she heard a much bigger sigh close beside her, and she noticed that the sheep's tails were waving up and down, looking somehow very miserable. The room seemed filled with one big sigh, and outside the winds appeared to have caught it up, and were carrying it onwards with them. Merle stopped and looked at Grunter Grim again, then instead of taking off the cloak, she wrapped it more tightly round her, saying softly to herself—

*"Defy, Deride, Desist, Deny,*
*Heed not a growl, or scowl, or sigh."*

Grunter Grim watched her closely, but said not a word. He stopped shivering and crying, his whole appearance seemed to change, and he was again the angry, sullen, mean little man. Then he gave Merle a withering glance of hatred and scorn, and walked out of the room.

Merle did not know what to do next. She did not feel much inclined to follow Grunter Grim, and yet she knew that she could do no good until she had made him give her the sealed packet. She was just making up her mind to have one

more really good search, when she noticed that
the little window had opened itself again.

" That clearly means that I am to get out of
this house, and I am very glad of it," said Merle,
and she stepped over the window-sill and out
into the garden.

She was preparing to make her way down the
crooked road when she heard a low chuckle close
to her elbow.   It was a very wicked chuckle, and
Merle turned quickly round, fully expecting to find
Grunter Grim at her side.

Instead of this, however, she found a little man,
or rather a boy.   He was fat, and looked as if his
clothes were much too small for him.   He was
dressed in bright green, and ugly enough he
looked.

As Merle turned round and faced him, he gave
a jump, as though he were frightened, and ran
against Merle, but as soon as he caught sight of
her face, he chuckled again.

" Beg pardon, Miss, I'm sure," he said, " but
I thought until you turned round that you were

Grunter Grim. However did you manage to get his cloak and hat?"

"Why do you want to know? Who are you?" asked Merle, for somehow she felt suspicious of the boy.

"Beg pardon," said the boy, grinning, "but I'm Johnny Green."

"Johnny Green! I seem to know that name," said Merle. "Are you one of the Rhymes?"

"Of course," said the boy, grinning again.

Merle felt very comforted when she heard that, for when she first saw him she had quite expected to find that he had something to do with Grunter Grim.

All at once the boy began laughing loudly, apparently without reason.

"You seem to be amused," said Merle, politely.

The boy laughed still louder. At last he managed to gasp out—

"It would be such fun, you know!"

Merle ventured to say she did not know what he meant.

I

" I want to play a trick on Grunter Grim, and you must help me," said the boy.

" I don't like Grunter Grim, and I don't like playing tricks," said Merle, "but tell me what it is. If it will help me to get what I want, and if it will be of use to the Rhymes, perhaps I might do it. Tell me what it is."

" Well, to begin with, you must give me the cloak and hat," said Johnny Green, beginning to laugh again.

" Oh, I am not likely to do that. I don't know enough about you to trust you with anything so precious," said Merle.

" Well, you know I am one of the Rhymes; didn't I tell you I was Johnny Green?"

As he spoke the boy came nearer to Merle, and took hold of the cloak.

" Johnny Green; I do remember the name, of course," said Merle. " ' *Who put her in? Naughty Johnny Green.*' Why, you're the boy that put Pussy in the well, ding dong bell. I won't have anything to do with you."

Merle pulled the cloak away from Johnny. It needed a hard pull, for he had taken firm hold of it, and evidently meant to get it.

Merle indeed was only just in time; in another minute he would have had it off her shoulders.

"You're a bad boy, Johnny Green; don't touch me. I won't look at you," she cried.

But something was happening to Johnny Green. He had begun to alter as soon as he touched the cloak. His green clothes became much darker, and he grew thinner. When Merle shouted to him to go away and not touch her, the person who stepped back and stamped his foot was no longer Johnny Green, but Grunter Grim!

"You thought to catch me in that way, did you?" said Merle. "You pretended to be a harmless Rhyme, and hoped to make me help you in your tricks."

"My cloak and hat, give them to me," said the little man.

"I won't give them to you. Now find me the

sealed packet which you stole," said Merle,
defiantly, for she was not a bit afraid of
him.

" I can't find the packet without my hat. Give
me my hat, and I promise you I will give you the
packet," begged Grunter Grim.

Merle hesitated.

" Well, give me the packet first," she said,
" and then you shall have the hat."

There didn't seem to be any way of finding it
without Grunter Grim's help, so she determined
to sacrifice the hat.

" You promise ? " said Grunter Grim.

" Yes," said Merle; but as she said it she shud-
dered, and then she knew that she had made a
mistake, but it was too late now.

" You've got the packet," said Grunter Grim,
dancing, " it is in the hat, stuck right in the
pointed top. Wasn't it a good place to hide it ?
Now give me my hat."

He tried to snatch it away from Merle before
she was able to get the packet out; but this time

she was too quick for him. She just managed to get a very small parcel out from the top of the pointed hat before Grunter Grim snatched it away from her, and giving one big jump, reached the door in the top attic, and disappeared inside the house.

## CHAPTER XI.

### MASTER RICHARD BIRD.

WHEN Grunter Grim disappeared with his hat, Merle felt almost inclined to cry. She fully realised, now that it was too late, how silly she had been. Still, she had acted as she thought for the best, for of course she had no idea that the packet she wanted was concealed in the hat.

"Well," said Merle, "at any rate I have done some good. I have the cloak, and nothing shall get that from me, and I have the packet. Perhaps if I find the king's name in that, he will be strong enough to get Grunter Grim's hat away. Now to see what is in the packet. I wish that I were in the babies' house, so that "—but Merle stopped, something very peculiar was happening.

The cloak which she had wrapped so tightly round her was spreading out. It seemed to be dividing into two at the back. Then one part wrapped itself tightly round one of Merle's arms

and the other round the other, and then she
began without thinking to move her arms out
from her side and back again. Suddenly she felt
herself lifted from the ground into the air.

" ' I am just like a bird.' "

" Why, I am just like a bird," she shouted,
with great delight. " I can fly! I can fly!"

And she was very much like a bird. If you
had seen her as she flew swiftly through the air,
you might have mistaken her for a big black crow.

Presently she found that she was above the long, low house in which the babies were, and she decided to go down there, and open the mysterious packet which she still held in her hand. She was anxious also to find Thomas Muriel, and tell him her adventures.

She closed her wings down by her side and gently dropped to the ground. The moment her feet touched the earth the wings became a cloak once more.

She was now standing in front of the babies' house, before the very same door by which she had entered the last time, but now that door was shut, and then it had been open.

At first, however, Merle was not disturbed by this, but when she tried to turn the door handle, to her surprise, she found it would not open, and though she pushed, and pulled, and knocked, and tapped, it was all no good—the door still remained tightly shut.

"This is the queerest thing," said Merle. "I thought with this cloak I could get anywhere—

I don't understand it at all. Never mind, perhaps the packet explains everything, and if I can't get inside why I must open it outside."

As she spoke, Merle began to look more closely at the mysterious packet which she had managed to get from Grunter Grim.

It seemed at first sight very much like a small brown paper parcel, and yet Merle could not find out how it was fastened, for there was no string tied round it, nor was it sealed. She tried to tear it open, but could not. She turned it first one way and then the other, pushed and poked, pulled and fumbled, but could find no beginning or ending to it, and above all, no opening of any kind.

She tried for a long time very patiently, but at last she began to lose her temper.

" This really is too stupid," she said, stamping her foot. " I have the packet, and now I can't get it open. This is one of Grunter Grim's tricks, of course. I wish I could get hold of him. I wish I were at——"

She got no further, for in an instant the cloak
had shaped itself into wings, and she felt herself
lifted from the ground. "I shall have to be
careful," she said, as she rose higher and higher
in the air. "It is quite evident that I have only
to wish to be at a place, and the cloak will take
me there. No wonder Grunter Grim was able to
get about so quickly, and to be everywhere at
once. Now the only question is, where shall I
go?"

She hesitated, but only a second, for just
then she felt something touching her nose. She
let her wings drop, and began to descend to
the ground, to get out of the way; but the
something seemed to be following, and she had
to flap her wings in front of her face to protect
herself. At last, by a good deal of flapping, she
managed to get above the something, and as she
looked down at it—still following her—she managed to make out that it was a small bird which
had been attacking her face.

As soon as she could, Merle dropped to the

ground, and just as the wings joined and again
became a cloak, the bird also reached the ground,
and hopped up to her.

He seemed much astonished when he looked
at her, and began to apologise.

" I beg your pardon for attacking you, but I
thought you were Grunter Grim, and ——" here
he paused, and began to flutter his wings as
though he were much distressed.

Merle did not know what to say, and waited
for him to continue.

At last, after flying rather close to her face,
he once more settled down on the ground and
began to speak again.

" Would you mind putting your hand over
your nose, so that I cannot see it ? I am sorry to
trouble you, but ——"

Merle began to laugh. " What a very queer
thing to ask me to do ! " she said. " Whatever
am I to do that for ? Who are you ? "

"My name is Master Richard—Master Richard
Bird—and unfortunately I am forced by Grunter

Grim to attack every nose that I see, and to try to pull it off."

"How curious!" said Merle. "Don't you think it is cruel of you?"

"It would be if I did it, but then, you see, I am only forced to *try* to pull a nose off, so of course I never do it," explained Master Richard.

Merle did not quite understand, but was afraid to ask any more questions, lest the bird should think her rude.

"Would you mind telling me if that is Grunter Grim's cloak? I suppose it must be," said Master Richard, after a minute's silence.

"Of course it is," said Merle, "and I have the packet too. I managed to get them both, but it is not much good, because I can't open the packet."

"Why not?" asked the bird. "You have the hat, I suppose, if you have the cloak. Use the hat to open the packet; it will open anything."

"But I haven't got the hat," said Merle, almost beginning to cry. "I gave the hat back to Grunter Grim."

" Well, that is a pity," said Master Richard. "Didn't you know that the cloak is of no use without the hat? for though the cloak will take you to any house, the hat only will get you inside. If you have the hat, you can open any lock, any door, any window, anything—even the parcel."

" Then I must get the hat as soon as possible," said Merle. " Won't you help me ? "

" Yes, indeed, I will, if you will keep your nose out of the way, and I'll get the four-and-twenty blackbirds to help, too," said Master Richard.

Merle stared at him. " Four-and-twenty blackbirds," she said to herself. " Richard Bird and my nose! What does it all mean ?"

Master Richard, however, took no notice of her, but flew as high as he could into the air, and began chirruping and whistling.

Close behind her Merle heard an answering chirrup, and in a minute a pert young blackbird perched himself on her shoulder. Then a whistle,

and behold there was a bird on the other shoulder; then a bird
flew on her head,
and another, and
another, and an-
other, until black-
birds seemed fly-
ing all round her.

At last Master
Richard stopped
whistling, and
came down to the
ground. He plac-
ed himself right
opposite Merle,
called to the black-
birds once more,
and they formed
a line behind him,
and then they be-
gan to sing.

"Blackbirds . . . flying all round her."

Merle only

listened for a while, then quite suddenly she too began to sing. She sang simply because she could not help it—she felt obliged to sing at the top of her voice:

> *"Sing a song of sixpence,*
> *A pocket full of rye,*
> *Four-and-twenty blackbirds*
> *Baked in a pie ;*
> *When the pie was opened*
> *The birds began to sing,*
> *Wasn't that a dainty dish*
> *To set before a king ? "*

The birds did not appear to mind at all; indeed, they seemed to enjoy it. Merle went on with the second verse, about the king being in the counting-house and the queen in the parlour, but when she sang,

> *" The maid was in the garden, hanging out the clothes ;*
> *There came a little dicky-bird, and pecked off her nose,"*

she found that the birds had stopped and she was singing alone. When she finished, all the blackbirds began to shout at her, "Shame! Tear her to

pieces! It isn't true! Shame!" It was evident
that somehow she had offended them, and they
were very angry. Merle tried to speak, but there
was too much noise. Then she shouted, but it was
no good. At last Master Richard stepped forward,
and at once there was silence.

"Blackbirds, be quiet, it is ignorance; she
means no harm," he said, and then he turned to
Merle. "I am sure you would not have sung the
last part of that song if you had known how it
offends us. I am Dicky Bird. I told you my
name was Richard, but sometimes I am called
Dicky. I am Dicky, and that day that I hurt
the maid—and, by the way, I did not peck off
her nose, though I'm sorry to say I tried to—I
was very much upset. It was partly Grunter
Grim's fault——"

"I understand," interrupted Merle, "and I
am so sorry. But I will never sing it again, and
you must help me to banish him. The first thing
to do is to get the hat. Let us quarrel no longer,
but all set to work."

# CHAPTER XII.

## A MYSTICAL RHYME.

AT the word of command from Master Richard all the blackbirds formed themselves into a circle round Merle, and they were just as quiet and polite as they had been noisy and rude before. They only spoke when they were spoken to, and indeed, took little part in the discussion. Merle and Dicky did all the talking, and at last agreed upon a plan of action.

It was arranged that all the blackbirds, with Dicky at their head, were to fly to Grunter Grim's house, get in, if possible, and look for the hat; and if not, to hover about, find Grunter Grim, and try to get some information from him.

Merle, meantime, was to stay behind and keep out of sight, for fear Grunter Grim should recognise her, and try to get back his cloak.

J

Everything being thus settled, Dicky Bird flapped his wings and flew upwards, crying "Forward!" All the four-and-twenty blackbirds followed his example, and soon Merle was left alone to await their return.

She made herself very comfortable on the stump of a moss-grown tree. As she sat down, she heard a voice singing softly—

> *"Little Miss Muffet*
> *Sat on a tuffet,*
> *Eating curds and whey."*

Merle sprang to her feet and looked round, but she could see no one. Then she looked again at the stump of the tree, and noticed that there was a small label fastened to one side of it, on which was written—

"MISS MUFFET'S TUFFET."

"This is very interesting," said Merle. "I wonder if the spider will come?"

"Of course he won't," said a voice just behind her. "Grunter Grim is the spider, and how can he come when you have the cloak? He is a prisoner!"

Once more Merle turned round, and this time a girl was standing in front of her. She recognised her as the girl she had seen at the meeting, and anyhow, she would have known who it was, because the girl's name was written on the label fastened on her dress.

"So Grunter Grim was the spider," said Merle. " I thought you didn't look the kind of girl to be frightened by a real spider."

" Frightened by a spider—no indeed. Let me tell you my story," said Miss Muffet.

" I suppose it is like all the others," said Merle. " Grunter Grim is the cause of all your trouble, is he not?"

Miss Muffet was just going to answer, when Merle saw two of the blackbirds flying towards them.

"Look, look!" she cried, "they are coming back. Now we shall get some news"

" News?" said Miss Muffet; " news of what?"

But Merle did not answer her, for by this time the blackbirds had reached the two girls, and had perched themselves on Merle's shoulders.

" Tell me—what have you seen or heard ? " said Merle.

" I went to the house," said Blackbird Number One.

" Just like *me*," said Number Two.

" And there I saw a window," continued Number One.

" *Just* like me," cried Number Two.

" And I looked in and saw Grunter Grim," went on Number One.

" Just *like*——" began Number Two; but Merle interrupted him.

" Do tell me a little quicker," she said. " Had he the hat on ? Did you see it ? Did you ask him anything ? And what did he say ? "

" ' No,' to the first question ; ' No,' to the second ; ' Yes,' to the third and fourth," shouted both blackbirds.

"I asked him where the hat was," said Number One.

"Just like me," said Number Two.

"And he said, 'Ha, ha, ha!'" said Number One.

"No, he didn't," said Two; "he said, 'The hats,' as if there were six or seven magic hats."

"HA! HA! HA!—THE HATS," said Merle, slowly; "what could he have meant?"

But the two blackbirds made no reply, they seemed to think they had done enough work for one day. They flew down from Merle's shoulder, and perching on Miss Muffet's Tuffet, tucked their heads under their wings, and went to sleep.

Merle was beginning to feel angry with them for being so stupid when she saw quite a number of their brothers flying towards her.

"Ah! here they come," she said to Miss Muffet. "Now, this time I will tell them what they saw, and try to get the news more quickly."

"I believe I begin to see what it all means,"

said Miss Muffet. " You have the cloak, and you are trying to get the hat."

" Hush!" said Merle, as twenty-two black-birds flew to the ground and hopped in front of her.

As soon as they were settled, without waiting for them to speak, Merle began—

" You went to the house."

" Just like me !" shouted each blackbird.

" And there you saw a window, and you looked in and saw Grunter Grim," said Merle, very rapidly ; " and he had not the hat on, and you didn't see it, and you asked him a question, and he said——"

All the blackbirds shouted at the top of their voices something, but, as they all spoke together, Merle could not understand a word.

" Say it one at a time," said Merle ; but the blackbirds took no notice of her, they just hopped on to the tuffet, and went off to sleep.

" Oh dear !" said Miss Muffet, " how tiresome of them.   What shall we do?"

"Never mind," said Merle, "here comes Master Richard—he will help us."

"Yes, that he will," said Miss Muffet—"only cover up your nose, my dear."

She only spoke just in time, for Master Richard flew straight at Merle's face, and would certainly have touched her nose had she not covered it up.

"I beg your pardon," he said—"but you know——"

"Never mind," said Merle, "give us the news."

"I have very little to tell, unhappily," said Master Richard. "I haven't found the hat, and though I saw Grunter Grim, he wouldn't answer any questions, and whatever I said to him, he only said, 'No one else can.' What he meant by that I don't know. Have the others come back?"

"Yes, but look at them," said Merle, dolefully. "They have all seen Grunter Grim, and he has said some nonsense or a bit of a sentence to each of them; but as they all shoute' together, I couldn't exactly make out what it was."

" Put all the bits together, and see if they make a proper sentence," said Miss Muffet.

" But the birds are fast asleep, they won't say it again," said Merle.

" I'll soon make them," said Master Richard. " That is a good idea, Miss Muffet."

Directly Master Richard called to them, the blackbirds woke up; when he called to them a second time, they all jumped to the ground ; and at the third call they formed themselves into a line in front of him.

" Now, Blackbirds," said Master Richard, " tell me what you each heard Grunter Grim say. Speak one at a time, clearly and distinctly."

Without a murmur, or even a " Just like me," the birds began—

" To me Grunter Grim said ' HA ! HA ! HA ! ' " said Number One.

" To me he only said ' THE HATS,' " said Two.

" To me ' SAFE,' " answered Three.

"To me he only said 'AWAY,'" said Four.

"When I spoke to him he said 'RIGHT,'" said Five.

"When I asked where the hat was, he said 'WELL HIDDEN,'" said Six.

"And when I said 'Is it lost?' he said, 'FOR EVER AND A DAY,'" said Seven.

"Stop a minute," said Merle, "I see something."

"Yes, so do I," said Miss Muffet. "Put those words together, and you get a rhyme."

"Of course you do," said Master Richard; "it's just what I expected. Listen.

> *"Ha! Ha! Ha! the hat's safe away,*
> *Right well hidden for ever and a day."*

"It doesn't tell us much," said Merle.

"Wait for the rest," said Master Richard. "Now, Number Eight, what did he say to you?"

"'DING, DONG,'" answered Eight.

"He only said 'THE' to me," said Nine.

"And only 'BELL' to me," said Ten.

" When I questioned him, he said, ' Of course I know,' " continued Eleven.

" And he said to me ' No use,' " said Twelve.

" I only caught the word ' In ' when he spoke to me," said Thirteen.

" And as far as I could make out, he said ' That' to me," said Fourteen

" I heard him say ' without the cloak,' " said Fifteen.

" And he called out ' Ho! ho! ho!' to me," said Sixteen.

" Two more lines of the rhyme," cried Miss Muffet, excitedly. " Listen, Merle.

> " ' *Ding, dong, the bell, of course I know,*
> *No use in that without the cloak, Ho! Ho! Ho!' "*

" Go on, go on," said Merle.

" To me he said ' Merle,' " said Seventeen.

" To me he whispered ' Stole,'" said Eighteen.

" And to me ' The cloak,' " said Nineteen.

" I heard the words ' From the poor old man,' " said Twenty.

" He only said ' SHE ' to me,' " said Twenty-one.

" And to me he said ' MIGHT GET,' " said Twenty-two.

" I heard him say ' THE HAT,' " said Twenty-three.

" And to me he said ' BUT,' " said Twenty-four.

" And that's all," said Merle.

" Wait a minute," said Master Richard, " you are forgetting what I heard. He said ' No ONE ELSE CAN ' to me."

" Now say the whole rhyme slowly," said Miss Muffet, getting more and more excited.

Master Richard pointed to one bird after the other, and this is what they said—

*"Ha! Ha! Ha! the hat's safe away,*
*Right well hidden for ever and a day.*
*Ding, dong, the bell, of course I know,*
*No use in that without the cloak, Ho! Ho! Ho!*
*Merle stole the cloak from the poor old man ;*
*She might get the hat, no one else can."*

"It isn't a little bit of good; it just tells us what we knew before," said Merle, in a very disappointed tone.

"It's a trick of Grunter Grim's," said Miss Muffet, very sadly.

Even Master Richard looked down-hearted. The Rhyme was, as Merle said, "no good at all."

Presently, however, just as the blackbirds were dropping off to sleep again, Merle called out—

"Stop! Perhaps the words would make another Rhyme if we took them in different order."

"You are clever," said Miss Muffet. "I expect you are right. Try them backwards."

But that was no good, it only made nonsense. Then they tried all kinds of ways, but could not get anything at all sensible. At last, just as Merle had made up her mind to give it up altogether, Miss Muffet had a brilliant idea.

"I expect the Rhyme begins with 'Ding, dong, bell,'" she said, "for that is Grunter Grim's favourite rhyme."

"Why didn't we think of that before?" said Master Richard.

"And perhaps, oh! perhaps," said Merle, excitedly, "the hat's hidden in the well. Do let us try to get the Rhyme once more."

They did try very hard. They made the blackbirds stand first one way, and then the other, they mixed them up, and made them shout until they were nearly hoarse, and at last they placed them side by side in this order, with Master Richard in the middle:—8, 10, 3, 13, 9, 6, 5, 4, 7, 17, 22, 23, Master Richard, 21, 18, 19, 20, 1, 24, 11, 14, 2, 12, 15, 16. Then they each said the word or words they had heard once through, and there was such a cry of delight from Merle, such a shout of joy from Miss Muffet, such a lively chirp from Master Richard, and such a twittering and chirruping from the four-and-twenty blackbirds! The secret was found out!

"Now, say your words once more," said Master Richard, and the birds shouted each in

turn, and this is how the Rhyme sounded this
time :—

> *" Ding, dong, bell,*
> *Safe in the well,*
> *Hidden right away*
> *For ever and a day.*
> *Merle might get the hat, no one else can ;*
> *She stole the cloak from the poor old man.*
> *Ha ! Ha ! Ha ! but of course I know*
> *That the hat's no use without the cloak, Ho ! Ho ! Ho !"*

Then came another cheer, and then Merle,
Master Richard, and Miss Muffet set off running,
flying, and jumping, to find the well and get the
hat.

# CHAPTER XIII.

## DOWN THE WELL.

MERLE found the well quite easily. With her magic cloak she moved through the air so quickly that Master Richard and Miss Muffet could not keep up with her, and they were soon left far behind. The well was surrounded by thick trees —so thick, that Merle could not help thinking, as she dropped gently to the ground, that she would never have been able to make her way through the bushes on foot, and that had she not had the cloak to help her, she would not have found the well at all.

It was very like an ordinary well—indeed, the only difference between it and most wells was that above it was fastened a very large bell, from which dangled a very long rope.

Merle knelt down on the ground and peeped

into the well. To her delight, she could not see any water in it.

"Hurrah!" she cried, "it will be easy to search that well thoroughly. I was wondering how I should be able to go underneath the water."

She wrapped her cloak round her, wished, and soon felt herself falling gently down, down, down. She reached the bottom quite safely, and at once began her search.

"It is a very large well," she said, as she felt her way about, for it was much too dark to see anything, "and the walls are certainly very damp."

The walls were very damp, though perhaps that was not strange. Every one expects the bottom of a well to be damp. Every one does not usually, however, expect the walls of a well each time they are touched to send out little jets of water, but that was happening in this well.

The water, too, rose rapidly, and in a little time it reached above Merle's knees as she stood in it.

"I see what is the matter," said Merle, slowly, " Grunter Grim means to try to drown me. It is not a bit of good, I mean to find his hat before I go up."

She moved about quickly, but the well seemed to grow larger, and the water was still rising rapidly.

It reached her waist. Should she give up the search ? Just then her foot knocked against something, something pointed. Could it be Grunter Grim's hat ?

Forgetting all about the water, she stooped down, seized hold of the point, and pulled. The hat—for it was the hat—was pushed very tightly into a hole in the wall.

" One more tug," said Merle.

But she did not give the one more tug, for she felt something pulling her from above, and before she could cry out or object in any way, she found herself lifted out of the water, out of the well, and on to the ground.

She struggled to her feet and looked about
K

indignantly, expecting to find Grunter Grim before her.

There was no Grunter Grim, only a very tall, very thin, very stupid-looking boy was standing staring at her. He carried a fishing-rod in one hand and a pail in the other, and he was trying to jerk the fish-hook out of Merle's dress, in which it was tightly fastened.

"Whatever did you do it for?" asked Merle, crossly.

"I thought that I had found the whale at last," said the stupid boy.

"Why, you *are* a Simple Simon," said Merle.

The boy frowned angrily.

"Whose fault is that?" he asked.

Merle looked at his pail, at his rod, and then at the ticket fastened on his coat. Sure enough, on it was written " Simple Simon "

"I beg your pardon," she said; "I didn't know."

"She found herself lifted out of the water."

"It was all Grunter Grim's fault," said
Simon; "I was——"

But Merle interrupted him.

"Then why did you fish me out of the well,
just when I was going to find his hat?" she
said.

"Oh, I am sorry! I am sorry!" said Simon.
"You see usually I spend all my time fishing in
this pail, but somehow to day I can do what I
like, and fish in other places."

"That is because I have Grunter Grim's
cloak," said Merle, "and he has lost some of his
power."

"Hurrah!" shouted Simon, and he threw his
cap into the air.

As it came down it caught in the bell-rope,
and at once the bell began ringing.

Ding, dong, bell! Ding, dong, bell!

"What a noise!" said Merle.

But it did not go on ringing very long, and
when Merle looked into the well once more, she
found that it was empty again, the water had all

run away. She wrapped her cloak round her, and turning to Simple Simon, said—

"Don't pull me out this time. I'm not a whale, you see."

"Then I had better be off," said Simple Simon. "I can't help fishing you out if I stay here."

Merle watched him disappear through the trees, and then went down, down, down to the bottom of the well again.

The walls seemed wetter than ever, and the water had risen to her waist before she had even found the point of the hat. It rose so rapidly that she was beginning to feel rather frightened. In spite of her fears, however, she felt very angry when once more she found herself lifted out, and dropped on to the ground.

"I told you to leave me alone," she said, impatiently. Then forgetting her anger, she began to laugh as she looked at the round smiling face of the boy standing over her.

He took off his cap, made a low bow, and said politely—

"*Who pulled her out? Little Tommy Stout.*"
And then he bowed again.

"I wish you had left her in," said Merle. "I
never shall find the hat if you and Simon keep
fishing me out of the well."

"So sorry," said Tommy, still smiling; "but
the fact of the matter is I thought you were Pussy.
And you'll excuse me mentioning it, but you didn't
seem to be thoroughly enjoying the water, though
you are not as wet as you might have been under
the circumstances."

"No," said Merle, "I wasn't enjoying the
water, and I am afraid I shall be drowned before I
can get the hat, the water rises so quickly."

"You don't mean to say," said Tommy, without even a little bit of a smile, "that you stayed
in the well when the water was rising."

Merle nodded.

"Then the only thing I wonder at is that
you are not drowned this minute. My dear young
lady, it is quite evident to me that you are not in
the habit of pulling pussies out of wells. If you

went into that well seven or eight times a day, as I do, you would know better than to venture in when it was full of water."

" It was empty when I started," said Merle.

" Then of course you did not ring the bell," said Tommy, " though I thought I heard it ringing just now."

" Is that the way you manage?" asked Merle.

" Of course," said Tommy. " What is the bell put there for ? I'll show you how it is done."

He jumped into one of the buckets, and seized hold of the bell-rope.

Ding, dong, bell! Ding, dong, bell!

The bell rang loudly all the time Tommy was in the well, and when he reappeared at the top once more, smiling as usual, he was perfectly dry.

" That's the way," he said, cheerfully; " but I think you are mistaken about the hat. I don't think it is there. I saw no sign of it."

But Merle was certain she was not mistaken, and taking hold of the rope and setting the bell ringing, she jumped into the bucket. In a few moments she reappeared with a smile of triumph on her face and the hat in her hand.

"What do you think of that?" she asked, as she put it on her head. " Now, Grunter Grim, you have indeed lost your power!"

Although she no longer held the bell-rope, the bell was ringing loudly, and all the birds in the wood were singing and trilling. Tommy was laughing heartily and shouting at the top of his voice " Hurrah!" and Merle trembled all over as she drew the parcel from her pocket.

She did not need even to touch the parcel with the hat, for as she drew it out she saw that it was open, and these were the mysterious words she found written inside it :—

> " *Who shall be Endom's king?*
> *A baby he*
> *Must always be ;*
> *For a baby is Endom's king.*
>
> " *What baby is Endom's king ?*
> *A baby that's glad*
> *When others are sad ;*
> *For contented is Endom's king.*

*" How to find Endom's king ?*
*The cloak he must wear,*
*Yet be free from care ;*
*For not all can be Endom's king.*
*" Who then is Endom's king ?*
*The baby that's glad*
*When others are sad ;*
*And his name it is Baby ——."*

Merle read it through aloud twice. She looked very puzzled, for there seemed to be something wrong with the last verse.

" I see what it is," she said at last.

" So do I," said Tommy.

" It's the same old story," said Merle.

" It's Grunter Grim," said Tommy; " he's scratched out the most important word in the whole rhyme."

" Yes, so he has," said Merle : " the word after 'baby' in the last line."

" Of course that was the name," said Tommy; " Oh dear! Oh dear!" and he seized hold of the bell-rope, and jumping into the bucket, disappeared down the well.

# CHAPTER XIV.

## HICKORY, DICKORY, DOCK.

As soon as Tommy had disappeared Merle turned away from the well.

" It's no use staying here," she said. " It is quite certain that there are no babies in the well; perhaps I had better go back to the baby-house."

She wrapped the cloak round her, and was going to wish, when she remembered the hat, and determined to try its power.

" If I can get through anything with this hat," she said, " I should think I can get through these trees."

Pulling the hat firmly down on her head, she prepared to push her way into the very thickest part of the wood which surrounded the well; but as soon as she reached the trees they seemed to move away from her. They crowded together on each side until there was quite a clear pathway,

and at last there were so few trees that at
the end of the pathway Merle could see a very
tall tower.   As she drew nearer to it, she noticed
that there was a large clock at the top of it,
and above the clock face were three letters—

## H. D. D.

" Well, at any rate, I may as well go up the
tower," said Merle.   " Perhaps I shall be able to
get a good view from the top."

It was easier, however, to say she would go up
the tower than to do it, for there did not seem to
be any door to it, or any way of getting into it.

" It's a good thing I have the hat," said
Merle.   " I suppose I must make a door for
myself."

She took the hat off her head, and was just
going to touch the walls of the tower with it,
when she heard a loud booming sound which
almost deafened her.   Whatever could it be?
Then she remembered the clock—perhaps it was
only the clock striking.

"They stood up on their hind legs and bowed solemnly."

She walked round to the front of the tower, and stared up at the clock-face. Now she noticed for the first time that instead of figures on the face, there were letters.

She began spelling out the letters slowly, " S M I R G R E T—" But she stopped, for she heard a great noise of scratching and scraping, and a sound of something tumbling, then it seemed as though nearly the whole front of the tower opened, and to Merle's great surprise three kittens came rolling out of the huge door. They rolled over and over until they were at her feet, when suddenly they stood up on their hind legs and bowed solemnly.

They were pretty kittens—so pretty that Merle longed to pick them up and cuddle them.

One was perfectly black, another quite white, and the third was a very handsome tabby. Each had a ribbon tied round its neck, and on the front of each ribbon was worked a name.

Merle tried hard to see what the names were, but she could only make out the shortest—the one tied round the grey kitten's neck, and that was "Dock." She was going to ask the names of the others, when all three bowed once more.

Then the black kitten stepped forward, and said, politely—

"Allow me to introduce myself—I'm Hickory."

"Then of course you are Dickory?" said Merle, pointing to the white kitten.

"Exactly so," said all the kittens together.

"And that's the clock," said Merle, pointing to the tower. "But what do the letters mean? 'S M I R G R E T N U R G'—doesn't seem to spell anything."

Hickory looked at Dickory, and Dickory looked at Dock.

"My whiskers!" said Hickory.

"After all this time she doesn't know," said Dickory.

"Rats and mice! who'd have thought it?" said Dock.

Then they all laughed, as only three little kittens can.

Merle went very red, she thought the kittens were rather rude. She turned round, and was going to walk right away, when Hickory said—

"Excuse me, but whose cloak have you got on?"

"Grunter Grim's," said Merle.

"And to whom does the hat belong?" asked Dickory.

"To Grunter Grim," said Merle again.

"Well, now look at the clock again," said Dock.

"Of course—how stupid of me!" said Merle. "I was reading it backwards. The letters spell 'GRUNTER GRIM'S.' I might have guessed that."

"So you might," said Hickory.

"Exactly so," said Dickory.

"Precisely so," added Dock.

Then the three little kittens joined paws and danced in a circle round Merle.

"Well, you are certainly the most remarkable

L

kittens," said Merle.    "I'm sure you never lost
your mittens, or began to cry."

The kittens stopped dancing immediately, and
put their paws behind their backs.

" Oh, you did, did you ? " said Merle, beginning to laugh.

" Tell her," said Hickory.

" Was it Grunter Grim ? " asked Merle.

" Exactly so," said Dickory.

" And I'm forgetting all about the Rhyme
and the King of Endom ; " and pulling her packet
out of her pocket, she read aloud the Rhyme to
the kittens.

" Now," she said, " can you guess the
missing word ? "

" Of course, it means that the king must
be a Rhyme Baby, you see that ? " said
Hickory.

" A Rhyme Baby ? " repeated Merle.

" Exactly so," said Dickory.

" A Nursery Rhyme Baby, not a real world
baby," said Dock.

"Well, I never thought of that," said Merle. "Of course it does. 'A baby who'll ne'er be a man' can't be a human baby. I never thought of that."

"And, of course, there are not many Rhyme Babies," said Hickory.

"Exactly so," remarked Dickory. "I've an idea."

"It's the first you ever had, then," said Dock, rather rudely. "You don't usually think for yourself."

"Oh, please don't quarrel," said Merle.

"Let us think," said Hickory.

The three little kittens, without any warning, stood on their heads. Merle was too much astonished to say anything, and waited patiently to see what would happen.

Presently Hickory gave a loud miaow, and immediately all three kittens again stood on their hind legs.

"I see," said Hickory, in a very mysterious ghostly voice, waving his tail in the

L 2

air, "I see a cradle in a wood on a tree-top, the bough is rocking, and the child is laughing.

> "*'When the bough breaks, the cradle will fall,*
> *Down will go baby, and cradle, and all.'*"

"I hear," said Dickory, "a voice singing a lullaby to a baby. Listen to the words."

Swaying from side to side, the three kittens began singing softly—

> "*Dance a baby diddy,*
> *What shall his mother do wid 'e?*
> *Sit in her lap, give him some pap,*
> *And dance a baby diddy.*"

As the lullaby died away, Merle looked at Dock, and waited eagerly for him to speak.

"And I see," said Dock, excitedly, "a lonely house in a lonely wood, a lonely baby in a lonely cradle, a——"

But just then the loud booming sound was heard once more from inside the clock.

"The mouse is up the clock—away!" cried Hickory.

"Exactly so!" said Dickory.

"Precisely so!" added Dock.

And away up the tower, as fast as their legs could carry them, scampered the three little kittens.

## CHAPTER XV.

### THE RHYME-SHOP.

"Now, that's a pity," said Merle, as she watched the three tips of the three tails disappear. "I wanted to ask them ever so many questions."

She wrapped the cloak round her, once more wished, and immediately felt herself floating in the air.

After flying a short distance, she saw the baby-house beneath her, and to her astonishment she found herself dropping down to the earth.

"This is curious," she said. "I wished to be at the Rhyme Babies' house, but perhaps they all live together."

Directly she reached the ground Thomas Muriel came hastening towards her, and as soon as he had heard the story of her adventures, he began to talk very fast.

"You have only one hour more," he said, "to

find the king, then there will be another meeting,
and you must go back to the earth. Let me help
you, and let us be very quick."

" Shall I give you the cloak ?" asked Merle.

" It is no good to me, I cannot wear it," said
Thomas Muriel,sadly ; " only a contented person
can wear it."

" Then I must find a contented baby, I suppose," said Merle.

" Of course, the Rhyme says so," said
Thomas Muriel ; " but don't waste any more time
in talking. Come this way."

Merle followed him down several passages,
and at last found herself in a large room.

In one corner of it was a cradle, and in the
cradle a baby was jumping up and down ener-
getically.

Some one in the room was singing—

*"Dance a baby diddy,"*

but Merle had not time to see who it was.

" Put the cloak round him," said Thomas
Muriel,

Merle obeyed. The baby was laughing and crowing at the top of its voice, but no sooner did the cloak touch him, than he began to cry and scream loudly.

Such a noise! Merle had never heard anything like it. She did not wait a moment, but snatching away the cloak, ran out of the room as fast as ever she could.

" He seemed a very contented baby," she said, as soon as they were safely outside.

" I can't make it out," said Thomas Muriel. " Say the Rhyme again."

Merle repeated it slowly—

> " *A baby that's glad*
> *When others are sad.*"

" That's it," said Thomas Muriel, " of course. That baby has never been glad when others were sad."

" Well, let us try another baby," said Merle. " Do you happen to know where the baby in the cradle on the tree-top is to be found ? "

" I know where to find her," said Thomas

Muriel, " but I am afraid she won't be any good, she hasn't been sad."

" Then don't you think a bough breaking, a cradle falling, and a baby and all tumbling down, would make you sad?" asked Merle, rather indignantly.

" Don't you see it says *when* the bough breaks," said Thomas Muriel ;. " and of course it never does break. It isn't likely it would. Why the baby would be killed."

" Well, I am very glad of that," said Merle. " All the same, I don't see what we are to do next."

Thomas Muriel looked puzzled.

" I wonder which baby Dock meant?" said Merle, quite suddenly. " Perhaps you know a lonely baby in a lonely house."

" No, I don't," said Thomas Muriel, sadly.

Merle began repeating the last verse of the Rhyme slowly—

> " *Who then is Endom's king ?*
> *The baby that's glad*
> *When others are sad ;*
> *And his name it is Baby* ——"

"Stop!" cried Thomas Muriel, "I see something. The baby's name must rhyme with 'king.'"

"Of course," said Merle. "Oh, don't you
know a name that will rhyme with ' king ? ' "

"I don't," said Thomas Muriel, " but I know
some one who does; come along quickly."

He seized hold of Merle, pulled her along,
and before she had time even to look round her,
pushed her in at the door of a small house, and
saying—"Now, be quick, I can't stop any
longer," ran away and left her.

Merle felt quite bewildered. She could not
speak, because she had lost her breath, but she
managed to use her eyes, and found that she was
in a small shop.

Behind the counter sat a very small person
with a very big head, writing busily. She was
so much occupied that she did not seem to see
Merle at all.

All round the room were shelves, with sheets
and sheets of paper packed tightly into them.
Each shelf had a number and a label.

One of these labels was quite close to Merle, and she took it up and looked at it. " Little Jack Horner" was written upon it, and as Merle peeped at the papers inside the shelf, she saw that each one was a copy of the Rhyme about Jack Horner.

She was pulling one out to see what the last line was, when she heard some one speaking to her, and turning round quickly, found herself in the presence of the Rhyme-Fairy.

She had a very small voice, so small that Merle could scarcely hear what she said.

" What do you want, little girl?" asked the Rhyme-Fairy; but before Merle could answer she went on, " There are plenty of rhymes to ' girl ' —hurl, whirl, curl, furl, for instance, but the proper one on this occasion is ' Merle.' "

Merle stared at her; then she managed to screw up her courage to say gently—

" If you please, I want a rhyme to ' king.' "

" Certainly," said the Fairy. " Rhymes to Order, you know," and she pointed to the sign above her head, on which was printed in large letters, " RHYMES TO ORDER. ANY RHYME FOUND ON THE SHORTEST POSSIBLE NOTICE. THE TRADE SUPPLIED, WHOLESALE AND RETAIL, BY THE RHYME-FAIRY."

Then she reached down a big fat book, marked " K," and began to turn over the leaves, talking quickly all the time—

" K—Ki—Kin—King. There you are ! Plenty of rhymes to ' king.' "

She showed Merle a long list of words, and ran her finger down it quickly.

" Is it comic poetry you are writing ? " she said, " because, if so, allow me to recommend ' fling,' the noun, not the verb, you know."

Merle shook her head.

" Oh, something sarcastic ! Then try ' sting.' No, something rather tender, perhaps ? Then I should strongly recommend ' cling,' or even ' ring.' I find ' cling ' in great demand."

Merle turned away, she did not understand

what the Fairy was talking about, and her precious minutes were flying fast.

She felt very sad. She did not want to go back to the world, leaving the Rhymes unhappy. But the little Fairy was still speaking to her.

"Won't you let me look at the whole line, Miss?" she was saying. "I feel sure I have something that will suit you, and answer your purpose."

Merle pulled the packet out of her pocket, and began to read the verse.

At once the Fairy's manner completely changed. She got down from her chair, pushed away her books and papers, and listened eagerly.

When Merle finished the first verse, she shouted—

"Go on! Go on! I'll help you. Down with Grunter Grim! I'm sick of Rhymes. Give Endom a king, and I'll make no more Nursery Rhymes. I shall be free."

Merle began the fourth verse, and as soon as

she finished the Fairy cried, "I see, I see—

> *' Who then is Endom's king ?*
> *The baby that's glad*
> *When others are sad ;*
> *And his name it is Baby BUNTING.'*

That's the word you want."

"Of course it is," said Merle ; " Baby Bunting
—B—— B——. He's always contented, though
*his father's a-hunting.*"

"*His mother's a-milking,*" cried the Fairy, excitedly.

"*His sister's a-silking and his brother's gone
to buy a skin,*" cried Merle. " He is contented
through trouble and care, that is quite certain ;
only let me find him—

> "' *The baby that's glad*
> *When others are sad ;*
> *And his name it is Baby BUNTING.'* "

But as she said the words she heard a wild
shout. It seemed as if there were numbers of
people repeating the words after her. She looked
up, looked down, the shop had disappeared, and
she was back again on the platform in the big hall.

## CHAPTER XVI.

### B—— B——.

BUT how different the Hall looked! No lamps were needed, for the whole room was flooded with sunlight. In each corner shone a big sunbeam, and in each beam hundreds of fairies were dancing madly. It scarcely looked like the same place, and Merle found it very difficult to believe that she really was in the big hall.

But the clocks were striking and the Rhymes were fast assembling.

Mistress Crispin and Jack and Jill were the first to arrive, and they were so busy talking together that they did not notice Merle.

" Just fancy, Mother," said Jill: " we really carried the pail full of water right up to the top of the hill, and we did not tumble down at all. What can it mean ?"

" What can it mean, indeed ?" said Mistress

Crispin. "What do you think has happened to me? The broth is no longer broth, it is once more——"

"Not roast beef and plum pudding," said Jack.

Mistress Crispin nodded her head.

"Hurrah!" shouted Jack. "We'll all come home!"

"Yes, they have come home," cried Bo-peep, as she came hurrying into the room. "What do you think I've found?"

"Not the sheep's tails?" said Jack Horner, who was just behind her.

"Yes, the sheep's tails—and on the sheep, too, my boy," said Bo-peep, triumphantly.

"Well," said Jack Horner, "to be a good boy I *will* try." Bo-peep stared at him.

"Can you say it?" she said, eagerly.

"Indeed I can," said Jack; "not once this morning have I said the other thing."

Just then Mother Hubbard, the Man in the Moon, Miss Muffet, and Boy Blue came into the Hall together.

Each one looked more surprised than the other.

"What does it mean?" said the Man in the Moon. "I ate the porridge, and it didn't burn my mouth."

"What has happened?" said Boy Blue, almost in the same breath. "I've found my horn."

"Look at my tools!" shouted Johnny at the top of his voice, as he rushed into the Hall towards the platform with a hop, skip, and a jump. "I've found my tools, now I'll get more than a penny a day."

The clocks were still striking, and the platform was getting more and more crowded.

And when the last clock struck twelve every Rhyme had arrived, and every one seemed overcome with astonishment and amazement.

On all sides there were heard whispers, cries, and shouts of "What has happened? What does it all mean?" Hickory, Dickory, and Dock were thinking hard, standing on their heads, and Simple Simon was shaking his head solemnly, as much as to say, "I don't understand it a bit."

M

At last Merle stepped forward and held up one hand. There was a loud cheer, and then perfect silence as she began to speak.

"I have found you a king," she said. "He is contented through trouble and care, and he will banish Discontent, he will banish Grunter Grim, and you will be happy for ever."

The Rhymes began once more to cheer.

"His name——" said Merle.

But at that moment there was a wild shriek, and Grunter Grim, without hat, without cloak, looking small, and mean, and miserable, came bounding into the room.

"My hat, my cloak, my power!" he said.

The Rhymes laughed, they were not a bit afraid of him.

"All gone," said Pollie Flinders; "you'll never spoil any more of my new clothes."

"Gone!" said Tom the Piper. "Yah! who stole the pig? Why, you! And who got beat? Why, me!"

"Quite, quite gone," said Hickory.

"Precisely so," observed Dickory.

"Exactly so," said Dock.

And the three little kittens joined paws, and danced round and round the miserable little man.

"Yes, they are gone," said Merle, "but I have not got them. Behold them there!"

Grunter Grim turned, the kittens stopped dancing, and they and all the Rhymes looked in wonder.

For there, in front of the platform, stood a cradle, and by it stood Thomas Muriel.

Merle stepped forward, lifted the baby out of the cradle, and held

The King.

him up in her arms. The cloak was wrapped
round him, and in his small hand he held the
magic hat. Yet he crowed and cooed, and
seemed perfectly happy.

The Rhymes cheered and shouted—

> *" The baby that's glad*
> *When others are sad ;*
> *And his name it is Baby BUNTING."*

For a few moments there was wild confusion,
and then Merle looked round for Grunter Grim.
He seemed even smaller than when he first came
into the Hall.

"Go, Grunter Grim !" cried Merle.

"Go!" cried Mistress Crispin, " and take that
with you," and she threw her birch-rod away from
her.

"Yes, go!" cried Jack and Jill, Bo-peep,
Humpty Dumpty, Pollie Flinders, Tommy Stout,
and all the other Rhymes.

But above the cheers and shouts a clear,
silvery voice was heard, and as Merle looked

towards the cradle, she saw a beautiful Fairy hovering above it. Her face was the most lovely that Merle had ever seen. It was so sweet, so pure, so calm, and so peaceful.

The Rhymes were hushed. They too were gazing at the beautiful Fairy, and they too were listening to her.

" I am the Spirit of Contentment," she said in her soft silvery voice; " henceforward Endom shall be the land of contentment, the land of peace. Go, Grunter Grim! Go, live in the world, you are not fit for Endom. Go, live with the people who call Nursery Rhymes nonsense ! "

There was a happy "coo" from Baby Bunting, and where Grunter Grim had stood there was only a little black heap.

The Hall was growing darker. The Rhymes seemed getting smaller.

Crash ! Bang ! Crash !

Merle rubbed her eyes.

" Such nonsense, nonsense ! staring at those

Rhymes.   No wonder the child dreams uneasily."

Was it Grunter Grim's voice?   No, Grunter Grim was banished.

What was it?   Merle rubbed her eyes again The Hall, and the beautiful Fairy, the Rhymes, Baby Bunting, all had vanished.   She was in her own little room, and Uncle Crossiter was standing by her bedside.   She looked up at him solemnly, and then said slowly—

" I suppose you have a bit of Grunter Grim in you ? "

Uncle Crossiter started.

" What is the child talking about ? " he said. " I thought she was very much excited when she knocked the screen over.   I will fetch her mother."

Merle watched him leave the room, and then looked at the screen lying on the floor.   Had she knocked it down ?   Had she been asleep ? and was it only a dream, after all ?

She felt quite bewildered.

As her mother came into the room she said solemnly—

" I wonder if the Rhyme Fairy will alter all the Rhymes, and make them end properly now."

Her mother looked at her; she began to think that Uncle Crossiter was right, and that the child was delirious.

But Merle saw the puzzled look on her mother's face, and began to laugh.

" I'm all right, mother," she said, " only I've had a wonderful dream. Let me tell you all about it."

And Merle told her all about it.

" Only you see, mother," she said, when she had finished, " Thomas Muriel never got his right body back again, so that there must be some boy walking about in a girl's body now. I wish I knew him. I mean her—no, I mean him. Don't you?"

But her mother only smiled and kissed her.

THE END.